CORNISH
SHORT
STORIES

CORNISH SHORT STORIES

A Collection of Contemporary Cornish Writing

Edited by Emma Timpany and Felicity Notley

Cover design © Vita Sleigh, www.vitasleighillustration.com

Vita Sleigh has asserted her right under the Copyright, Designs and Patents Act 1988, to be identified as illustrator of this book cover design.

Woodcut illustrations © Angela Annesley, www.ravenstongue.co.uk

Angela Annesley has asserted her right under the Copyright, Designs and Patents Act 1988, to be identified as illustrator of these woodcut illustrations.

First published 2018

The History Press
The Mill, Brimscombe Port
Stroud, Gloucestershire, GL5 2QG
www.thehistorypress.co.uk

ISBN 978 0 7509 8355 6

Typesetting and origination by The History Press
Printed in Turkey

CONTENTS

INTRODUCTION

AS WE put together this collection, we were determined that the stories we chose would not simply reach for familiar tropes – rugged cliffs, romantic beach scenes and pasties – but would have sprung from felt experience. They needed to be true both to their writers and to Cornwall. When a seagull does fly in from the wide blue yonder, as in Rob Magnuson Smith's masterful story 'Sonny', it instantly becomes both more than itself and exactly what it is, inscrutable behind its yellow eyes.

Writers are often solitary but can flourish when brought together. We both feel fortunate to have discovered Telltales, a live literature event based in Falmouth, where writers share their work and socialise over a drink or two. It was through Telltales that Nicola Guy from The History Press – herself from Cornwall – found us and invited us to edit this new anthology. Nicola had some rules for us to follow: the writers included must be Cornish by birth or upbringing or must live in Cornwall. Cornwall also had to feature as a setting in the stories themselves.

The work of this current generation of Cornish writers is hard to classify; nothing is clear-cut in this far-flung place. The many legacies of Cornwall's industrial and maritime past still visible in the region have informed a number of the stories. Elaine Ruth White's 'The Hope of Recovery' takes us diving deep to a wreck beneath the waves of our dangerous coastline. Sarah Thomas's

'Ballast' pays tribute to Cornwall's presence on the world map in the great age of sail, a time when explorers and naturalists, including Charles Darwin, passed through Falmouth's natural deep water harbour. The stories create their own map of Cornwall: from the Tamar to the Helford, from Bodmin to Penzance, from Launceston to Zennor.

During the submission process, many retellings of traditional Cornish tales surfaced. Emma Staughton's 'The Siren of Treen' – a melodic reworking of 'The Mermaid of Zennor' told in three voices – stood out, as did emerging writer Anastasia Gammon's 'The Haunting of Bodmin Jail', an original and witty take on the classic ghost story.

Given Cornwall's long history as a source of inspiration for artists, we felt the visual design of the book should reflect this. Elemental forces in the cover design by Vita Sleigh and in the woodcut illustrations by Angela Annesley resonate between the contemporary and the traditional, rather as modern life and a rich literary heritage feed into the writers' words. Vita described the inspiration behind her design as follows:

> My approach was to use colours which I felt expressed the essence of Cornwall: wild, often grey (the sea in winter, stark cliffs, the turbulent skies), earthy with splashes of colour (the bright green that mosses can be, the yellow of gorse flowers, the deep almost tropical blues of the ocean on those rare but gorgeous Cornish days).
>
> The image of the wind-blown tree was something I came back to again and again in drawings. It is what I thought of first when I saw the brief. I liked the idea that the tree has been shaped by the Cornish landscape and weather, in very much the same way that the writers will also have been heavily shaped by living in this sometimes harsh but beautiful area of the world.

Whilst Cornwall's past never feels far away, Candy Neubert's 'Beginning Again' is set very much in the present, detailing the intricacies of a father–son relationship on an idyllic Cornish beach. The liminal space between land and sea is also the setting for 'The Kiss' by Philipa Aldous, where a girl and boy walk together, full of anticipation for the moment that will surely come. More complex relationships are the focus of Tom Vowler's exquisite and moving short story, 'An Arrangement', and S. Reid's beautifully wrought tale, 'Too Hot, Too Bright'. The shifting boundaries between fiction and poetry are explored in Cathy Galvin's richly layered prose poem, 'The Maple is in Blossom'.

One of the defining characteristics of Cornwall is its separateness: there is joy to be had in crossing the Tamar from east to west. We are delighted that Tim Hannigan has allowed us to include in the collection his inspired, numinal piece, 'On the Border' – a deeply-felt exploration of place and time.

We've chosen to open this book with Katherine Stansfield's poem 'Talk of Her'. The 'her' in question is Dolly Pentreath, the last native speaker of the Cornish language.

Emma Timpany and Felicity Notley
Cornwall, 2018

TALK OF HER

KATHERINE STANSFIELD

They say she spoke no English as a maid
hawking fish in Mousehole. They say

she was found by the language man
as if she was lost, that the day he came

she was raging. He thought her curses Welsh
at first, then caught something else.

A witch, they say, and Cornish
her tongue for witching. They say

she was wed and unwed. They say
there was a child, a girl, though some

say a boy, say he died. By the end
she'd prattle anything for pence. They say

she was the last to speak it, but listen –
there's others here still talking, and when

I dug her up last week, forty-seven feet
south-east from the spot they had marked, her

with three teeth in that cracked and famous
jaw, I tell you, she spoke just earth and water.

ROARING GIRL

ALAN ROBINSON

SHE WAS the first person I saw at the festival as I entered the tea room, flooded with light from the domed glass ceiling, which showed fluff on her black velvet jacket and britches. She looked up as I approached.

'Is it Eileen?' I asked.

She smiled. 'Aileen.' Emphasising the A.

'I'm Jack.'

'Sit down.'

'Can I get you a tea or something?' I asked. She was sitting at the table like a sprung coil, looking as if she wanted to get away quickly.

'I'd rather have ale,' she said. 'Or better still, mead. There must be loads of mead around these parts.'

I couldn't place her accent, which sounded like Suffolk mixed with cockney and even some Irish. Nor could I tell her age. She looked girlish yet old, prematurely grey hair bobbed like a boy's.

She was both dandyish and slovenly: her ruffled lace shirt matched the velvet suit perfectly, but was a bit torn.

'I'm sure we can get mead. Follow me.'

Her eyes lit up, a burnished blue, and tiny dimples appeared in her cheeks.

'Now you're talking.'

'Have you been here long?' I asked as we walked down the hill from the tea room to the meadows, passing the main house where early festival machinations were taking place on the green outside, lots of women in wellies with Cornish accents bossing men about. It was understatedly alternative.

'An age,' she said.

'I'm sorry. My train was a bit late. Then I walked straight past the entrance to Port Eliot. It's more or less a hole in the long garden wall.'

'Which one of these tents has the mead?' she asked.

'The big one,' I gambled. I knew it was the beer tent, but not if it had mead. It did.

'You're a star,' she said, when I handed her the glass.

'Cheers.'

'This is a big show,' Aileen said. 'I've never seen so many people in a tent except at Royal Regattas.'

'Have you been to many?' I asked.

'A few,' she said. 'You have to. I get on quite well with some of the courtiers. They say the Queen likes me.'

'Thanks for meeting me,' I said. 'I've brought a CD which explains a bit about myself and the story. I thought it might help to listen to it when you've got a moment. I know you'll be busy here.'

She took the disc, turned it over with a blank look and put it on the bar. She then put her mead glass on it.

I didn't know what to say. I sipped my beer, spluttered into it, then said, 'I also have the story in print,' and took a copy of my book's introduction from my bag.

'Manuscript: that's what I'm used to. It's a bit thin though,' she said. 'Did you write it yourself? Maybe you should get help.'

I welcomed these put-downs as par for the course with star-rated literary consultants, as well as, if I'm honest, the dominatrix-ish frisson I sensed between us.

'Anyway, I'll have a look at it later. Tell me a bit about yourself,' she said.

I summarised my patchy writing career, titivating the most promising bits, and hoping to sound edgier than my subject matter.

'You didn't say anything about money, like what you were paid last, or what you wanted for this, but if you're a new boy I guess you just have to take the crumbs, am I right?'

By this time I'd truly lost my voice. I nodded.

'Thanks for showing me the mead house. I'll have a look at this tonight.'

'Thank you. I hope you enjoy it. Where shall we meet?' I called, as she moved off.

'Here, same time tomorrow.'

That night I tried to find and bump into her. Port Eliot's not so big that it couldn't quite easily happen. I looked for her velvet suit, but as it grew dark that was difficult even in the beer tents, and I hoped I would just run into her on a path through the trees, or on the moonlit walk along the riverbank. I came across only lovers and midnight swimmers, unaware of my presence, so that by the end of the night I began to feel like a ghost.

I wondered if she'd read my manuscript by now, and if it was a hit, or if she'd binned it and wouldn't turn up on Saturday to give me feedback.

After midnight passed, I gave up hope and followed the raised voices and slews of people heading for the Walled Garden. Under a marquee at the far end an Irish band was mixing every kind of world music to an Irish backbeat, the yells and whoops of performers and crowd growing more insistent as I came near. It was cold on the edge of the crowd, and to get warmer I pushed through until I was a couple of rows from the front. There she was, tambourine in one hand, a drink in the other, still in her black velvet suit, shirt collar undone, a determined look in her eye as she kept time. It was a family affair, and she seemed to be part of it, or a close friend, winking at a young girl guitarist in the band who was a little hesitant, urging her on. The song finished unexpectedly on an upbeat, the discipline of the finish taking the audience, including me, by total surprise. I blinked twice, and when I focused again, after my eyes had swum from woodsmoke and beaconing stage lights, Aileen had gone. There was a gap next to where the young girl musician stood with her guitar, looking lost. A lostness I shared.

It was pitch black away from the lighted tents. I walked along pathways beneath trees, numb and still exhilarated from the music. As the sounds everywhere damped down, there was nothing to do but find my tent and sleep.

Before I was due to meet Aileen the next day, I went to a writers' open mic, a semi-serious affair in a small tent in a grove of trees. I thought it would help me loosen up before my meeting. She was there, in an identical velvet jacket and britches, this time bottle-green, reciting a pub-song-cum-verse-drama, which reminded me of women blues singers whose records I'd heard from the 1920s, a riot of double meanings and sexual innuendo. It was a Rabelaisian hoot. She went down well, sandwiched between a couple of gawky lads whose stories were of self-loathing and self-love.

I followed her down the slope away from the trees, glad to see she was heading for the mead tent where we'd agreed to meet.

After getting drinks, I was about to ask if she'd been able to read my piece, when she said, 'The first thing is that you should stop writing about yourself, for Christ's sake. Choose someone famous or mythical, and forget prose. Why isn't it in at least iambic pentameter? And it has to be a play; at the moment it's like a long letter to no one. What do you say to that?' She took a sip of mead.

Dry-throated, I spluttered back that I respected her opinion but was trying to do something experimental with the prose.

'We all resort to a bit of loose prose every now and again, even Will Shakespeare,' she said. 'But plays are what entertain people. Think about what I've said. We'll talk some more, but now,' she drained the mead, 'I have to go and see the Queen.'

I followed her at a distance after she left the tent, out of sheer curiosity. I knew the Queen couldn't actually be there, even though she looks as good in wellies as the next person.

When I caught up with Aileen she was bowing to the Queen of Hearts in a children's pageant in the woods. She said, 'Majesty, may I have your ear?' and whispered something, after which the Queen pronounced: 'Clear the court, we must see a play!'

Aileen performed a one-woman play within a play about two star-crossed lovers and their goblin aides, both funny and moving, enthralling the kids and their mums and dads and me.

Afterwards I caught her eye, as she watched the end of the pageant from the far side of the audience. I smiled. She saw me, but turned away and walked towards the river.

That night I blotted her out, and her critiques. I told myself they were the rattling of an East End trendy who never set much of a foot outside London. Why come to these things and agree to see budding writers if you had no intention of nurturing them? For the free invite, no doubt, and the expenses. I got into Guinness, which simultaneously helped with the blotting out and made me feel more substantial.

I ended up at a gig in the music tent, which I came to halfway through. I could have sworn it was Bob Dylan in his Nashville Skyline period but on the way out heard someone say, 'He was just like his dad,' so surmised that it had been Dylan's son. I headed for the riverside walk, entranced by the fairy lights and thinking – still gobsmacked by the Dylan Junior gig – of reincarnation.

I got lost and stumbled on an open-air cocktail bar in a glade that played soul to die for. I sensed Aileen had been there – or maybe I just sensed her everywhere that weekend – and got to dancing and drinking with two women of Aileen's generation. They knew the moves. We had a good laugh, took selfies. I found for some reason I'd drunk myself sober and went back to my tent to re-read my manuscript. At that hour, approaching early dawn, it alternated between being genius and dross, often on the same page.

Wide awake and restless, I headed for the river across the meadows. The estuary birds would reassure me with the inhuman prescience of their calls; it had worked before.

The open-air cinema screen was still up, though now it was a blank white sheet, and a few all-night stragglers were still winding one another up with tall stories and meanderings among the wisps of mist suspended above the waterside.

Along the estuary there was a boathouse towards which I was walking. As I got near, I saw a boat swinging fast, driven by oars, headed for the boathouse. It glided in, and Aileen stepped forward to the end of the jetty. I hadn't seen her until the last minute, recognising first her bottle-green velvet of the day before, and then her boy's hair, as she stepped gingerly into the boat. I wanted to hurry and say goodbye, or please ring, both of which would have been equally inappropriate. She was going to wherever she'd come from, in the Hollywood manner in which she seemed to do everything, and she hadn't given me her card.

I walked back to the tent wearily. The manuscript was on its back, the last page turned over underneath it. There was some handwriting on the page, in a scruffy, spidery, blue-inked script. It said: 'Look me up if you're in London. I'm the original Roaring Girl. You can find me at the Mermaid Tavern in Fleet or my lodgings at Cheapside.'

Her last joke, I thought.

Next day, on the train out of Port Eliot, I was flipping through the photos on my camera. I came to the one I'd selfied at the cocktail bar after midnight and stopped. There were three women in the photo, one at the back with short bobbed hair, barely visible. It could only be her.

When I got home I Bluetoothed the photo to my computer and blew it up. The third woman had gone. But I had an email from the writers' consultancy I had contacted before the festival, which contained a profuse apology from them that Eileen had been unable to come to the festival, and would I send them my manuscript by email?

I emailed back to say that I had decided to write a play.

AN ARRANGEMENT

TOM VOWLER

IT IS one of those late summer evenings only Cornwall can yield – heady and languid, yet the county's slender form determining that the air will always be brackish, nautical, wherever you are. The garden's drowsy scent marshals in me nostalgia for the dozen or so Augusts we have spent here, seasons laid down deep in the brain's circuitry, more felt than known. Of droning bees, drunk on one of the colossal lavenders behind the old rockery, the day's heat subsiding yet still irrefutable. I picture the summerhouse – where swallows nest each year, where we would converge as afternoons lapsed, to imbibe each other's days – its exterior, I am told, in disrepair. And beyond this, quilted fields with hedgerows of yellowing hawthorn, the sparrow-haunted rowan richly berried, fragrant walks that should have been more prized at the time.

The low sunlight illuminating my wife's shoulder as she sits at her dressing table is somehow both mellow and scalpel-sharp – some trickery of the new medication, I suppose, which, whilst inhibiting some of the pain, distorts reality a few degrees. She is precise in her movements, a well-honed routine to enhance a beauty that was, she insists, late to flourish and which is only now perhaps beginning to wane. Men age so much better, she is prone to say accusingly, although perhaps there is altruism here, in case on some level I am still preoccupied with how handsome or otherwise I remain. I want to speak, to deny the reminiscing further indulgence. Not because of her imminent departure, an exploit that has occurred monthly for the past year; but because there is something to be marvelled at in this dance we are able to perform – it would be simple for her to get ready in another room – as if my involvement, albeit one of mere observation, is somehow vital, consensual. Some months she even solicits my thoughts on a particular dress, a combination of jewellery I think works best, and I advise with due sincerity, delicate in my judgement, fulsome in praise. Perfume, though, is her realm alone, as if it speaks to a level of intimacy neither of us can endure, its selection seemingly flippant, a final flourish of decoration rather than the olfactory manipulation it aspires to be. Whether she imparts more scent than at the times we dined out together is hard to say; perhaps further adornment takes place in the taxi, a courtesy extended to me, one of several that have formed unbidden.

'You can ask me anything and I will tell you,' she said at the start. 'I know.'

And I have been tempted. Not from a rising paranoia or raging jealousy. More that I wonder if hearing such detail would arouse me on some level, allow a vicarious lust to play out. But I don't ask. As lovers in our thirties, I would have torn open any such rival, or at least threatened to, confronted him with animalistic fury before collapsing a tearful wreck. Such confrontation is beyond me now, but I sense no real desire for it. I am not so naïve as to mistake this for some Zen-like enlightenment, or worse still a Sixties openness to communal loving. I always wondered how that played out in reality, unadulterated by the rose-tinting of hindsight.

Was everyone who partook accepting of such frivolous hedonism, the sharing of orifices and organs, or was homicidal behaviour only kept at bay narcotically?

'Are you okay?' she asks. 'You seem distant.'

'I was just thinking,' I lie. 'Do you regret not having children?'

This isn't a fair question and could be construed as my attempting to mar her evening.

'Oh, darling, we've spoken about this.'

'I know, but you might have changed your mind.'

We were trying, right up until I became ill, which I suppose was rather late in life, at least for a woman. Careers had consumed us, the time never right. And then when it was: not enough blue lines in the little window. Tests showed no reason for our fallowness; it was simply a matter of perseverance, of sending enough seed swimming in the right direction. But the next batch of tests we endured – I endured – were of another order entirely.

'I'm content,' she says. 'I don't really think about it these days.'

Absent of all segue she speaks of the dinner awaiting me, cauliflower cheese, that she'll bring it in as she leaves. I make a joke about it being my turn to cook, but it's an old, well-worn line and goes unacknowledged.

'You've got your baclofen,' she says.

'Yes.'

'And you can take more naproxen at ten o'clock.'

'All two of them.'

Six months ago, when my mood found a new nadir, I began hoarding pills, with no more intent than to experience the sense of control it offered, some small reclamation of autonomy. Ever since she found them, their administration has been piously governed.

'You never ask me,' I say.

'What you want for dinner?'

'Whether I regret not having children.'

She sighs, a minute outbreath escaping despite herself.

'Can we talk about this when I get home?'

'Will that be before or after the sun is over the yardarm?'

I can't help myself. I don't even feel the level of spite it implies; it's as if I want to try it on – being a shit – like a jumper.

'I can't cancel now. We agreed. If you don't want me to go, you have to give me a few days' notice. It's courteous.'

This word seems to me inappropriate, their arrangement requiring a more squalid lexicon.

'I want you to go,' I say. 'I can sort myself out if you pass me some tissues.'

'Please don't be crude.'

It's true, I can just about, still – yet the thought fills me with weariness, the exhaustion of the thing, my mind the only reasonable place for sex to occur these days, and then only from habit. In the early years of incapacity we continued to make love, content in its gesture however unsuccessful the deed itself. And later, when this became impossible, she would use her hand, whisper lewd contrivances that led more to despondency than climax. Abstaining came wordlessly, a relief to us both.

And so my emasculation was complete. A man, in any true sense of the word, no longer. Whilst hardly the athlete, it has always been the loss of physical rather than cerebral activity that I've felt more keenly. Who'd have thought batting at ten or eleven, plus eight overs of regulation off-spin for the village side, ranked higher in my sense of worth than an associate professorship? Nothing like total debilitation to provide a little perspective.

The blurred vision came at the end of a stressful week, where rumoured redundancies became reality, our department likely to bear the brunt, and so the early symptoms were neatly aligned with events at work. Medicine, I have learned, is a patient creature, never rushing to judgement, content in the knowledge time will out. And so a series of hoops must be passed through, each one narrowing, each one ruling out potential, less condemning causes. None of this was helped by my mild but well documented hypochondria, which in the end even I clung to. Tingling or numbness?

Almost certainly nothing of concern, came the counsel. Fatigued? Aren't we all? Even the disturbed balance prompted only rudimentary scrutiny, blood tests, talk of an MRI. But after the first seizure a neurologist thought it prudent to tap my spine for some of its fluid, a joyous procedure, which suggested my body, far from suffering the slings and arrows of modern life, had in fact turned on itself. Later a new vocabulary evolved: bedsores, converted bathroom, managing expectations.

My wife stands and checks herself in the mirror, turning ninety degrees left then right, a look of satisfaction rather than vanity.

'I'm sorry,' I say, and she crosses the room, kisses my forehead, the Chanel still young, yet to blend with her own scent.

'If you're awake when I get back, I can read to you if you like.'

We are tackling my favourite Márquez, all 450 pages, most of which I won't remember, at least not this time round. But the essence of the book lingers in the suburbs of my mind, and so despite my attention wavering every few lines, there is still pleasure to be had. Pleasure especially in the sound of the words, my wife's voice a blend of honey and whisky, a balm no painkiller can rival. I wonder what texts the students have been given this term, what anodyne classics have been selected for their enrichment, novels chosen by committee to illustrate technique or theme, rather than to delight in. A couple of colleagues visited in the early days, bearing gifts and conversations that groaned with formula, office gossip their stock offering. Better off here, they would say, away from it all. Certainly I was accommodated for in those final days at work. Reasonable adjustments, as they're termed, were made as symptoms advanced: a parking space, pressure on fire doors eased, reduction of hours. I worked from home when possible. I knew all my work was re-marked, that I was just humoured in the end.

My wife moves the Márquez onto the bed, placing it in the space she will later fill, a promise of sorts. I smile, knowing the pills will render me beyond storytelling later tonight. In her absence I will listen to the radio, a surprising source of company that I've neglected most of my life. During the worst relapses, when mobility is nothing but fantasy, entire days can be built on the scheduling of programmes from around the world.

I try to remember the first occasion the matter of her taking a lover came up. Curious verb that, more something you associate with a hobby, the taking up of a pastime. Which lover would madam like to take? Have you browsed our online options? Just click Add to Cart when you're ready. I know nothing of him, no particulars beyond a handful of unsolicited revelations: age (around ours), profession (middle management), marital status (widowed). So he at least waited, I thought.

'Just tell me he doesn't play golf,' I said. 'I couldn't stand that.'

They met at badminton, or yoga, I forget now. He knows the score, of course, knows our situation. Presumably they still interact at badminton or yoga, but dinner and its attendant digestifs are kept strictly to the second Friday of the month, the first couple of which remained platonic, if I read between the lines correctly. She used his name more, was how it started, the word registering subliminally until one day its utterance became frequent enough to jar. And then came the conversation, the one you never conceived of midway through your marriage vows or on honeymoon as you coiled and writhed and devoured one another. A mature tête-à-tête, one that addresses base needs, that purports to be pragmatic, but in itself is enough to crush you. There would be no question of anything else, we agreed. Our bond was beyond severing, half a lifetime's narrative to this footnote, this loveless frisson. Like servicing the car, it helped to regard it. I could request its cessation at any time, and yet I have begun to cherish the mornings after, when she lies by my side and silently strokes my face deep into the day. It's as if she returns in need of forgiving, though no such exchange takes place. And then it's done for another month and I can almost forget about it.

She brings in dinner, checks I'm okay to feed myself, which sometimes I'm not.

'My taxi's here,' she says, and now I think about it I can hear the rapid tolling of the diesel engine, this vessel of sin, this transporter of goods. I wonder what the drivers think as they drop her off at the same restaurant, this woman who sports a wedding ring yet is always alone. Do they speak among themselves about this fare, about the house in the adjacent village they collect her from in the early hours?

'I will always have my phone on,' she once said, in reference to my physical rather than emotional needs. 'If you text I will come straight back. He understands this.'

Very good of him.

When sufficiently strong I like to revisit in my mind our first few years together, conjure as vividly as possible our trip to Tuscany, to Connemara, moments within moments kept alive by their rehearsal, my senses fed sound and colour and smell, words re-enacted. Done well my mind can even trick itself, escape its cage for a few minutes. I remember the time I fell in love with her, the exact second as new lovers in our twenties. We'd taken a small cottage on the Gower, and out walking one morning came across a table of free-range eggs for sale, below which was an honesty box. We had no money, but cooking up those eggs for breakfast was all we could think about. I suggested we just take some, that worse crimes happen all the time, but she insisted we write an IOU note, posting it in the box. After we ate them she walked back the few miles to settle up.

My wife kisses my cheek, tells me not to get into any trouble while she's out.

'I plan to have an ASBO before you return,' I say.

She's almost at the bedroom door when I speak again, the words sounding so plaintive they almost disgust me.

'Eat with me tonight.'

She looks hard at me, gauging the words, my face, to assess if it's still part of the banter. I lower my head like a child asking to take a puppy home.

'Please.'

And we remain there in bloated silence, the spoils of a marriage charging the air between us, and as I stare down at my stricken being I want to say I am still me, the same collection of particles and molecules and memories, still more than this shape-shifting abomination can ever reduce me to. I am more than the sum of my broken parts and I thought I could share you but I can't.

Instead I ask her if this year's swallows have left.

BEGINNING AGAIN

CANDY NEUBERT

She was coming straight up the beach towards him.

Through half-closed eyes, his head propped up against his ruck-sack, he watched her come. In silhouette at first, the kind of shape you just knew wasn't English, couldn't be English, but you couldn't say why. Hair plastered back slick and wet off her face.

She came right up and stood over him, flicking water over his hot skin. Hey, he laughed. She lifted her towel, shaking it out like a sheet over a bed, lying down with a grunt. He felt the cool coming from her, saw tiny droplets drying on her neck – Sonya, his mate, his life's woman.

'Mm … now I'm hungry,' she said, not opening her eyes. He was, too. He sat up slowly, sun dizzy, and reached into the rucksack. Here it was, the container she always filled to the brim. He raised a corner of the lid and out came the smell of food, olives and onion – just as the small figure of the boy crossed his line of vision, still quite far off, heading his way.

The path went straight up from Porthcurno and he took it two steps at a time. Not really steps but boulders and cliff straight up from the car park, just the way to get going on a cool morning. They'd soon be warm and the mist would clear; it was only a sea mist. He positively sprang all the way, pretty fit for a businessman, an office chap.

When the path levelled out, he waited for Daniel. It was an inviting path, gorse on either side, beaten earth sprinkled with rabbit droppings, gulls laughing overhead. But he kept still and waited patiently. He was so effing patient. But Daniel wasn't in sight.

Finally.

If shoulders could talk.

If shoulders could talk, the rucksack on Daniel's back would shrivel up and die. As if towels were heavy. Bulky, yes, but not heavy. He should try the picnic, if he wanted heavy. Also, Fuller had the surfboard, which was fair enough; his arms were longer. But Daniel was young and strong. They did sports training at school, didn't they?

The boy climbed the last bit and came to a halt five yards away, his eyes fixed on his shoes.

Patience, mind. Fuller held his tongue and set off again. A fresh scent came from the pink flowers in the grass under the gorse, while the mist ripped back off the cliffs before his eyes – what luck, when it might have come in thick and spoiled everything.

They did sports training and next year Mandarin, of all things. He'd asked Daniel about it yesterday, about the new school. The boy made a face, sticking his tongue over his front teeth. They're all tossers, he said. He'd wanted to go to a school in Devon where they taught tractor driving.

But they were going to have a day today, a great day. They were here, damn it. The sun was coming out and everything was sorted.

A kestrel rose and hung in the air, over to the right. Fuller put his fingers in his mouth and whistled, and the boy raised his head.

'What?' he yelled.

'Kestrel!'

'Uh.'

Now, five hundred yards ahead, a gate – it had to be the right place, the path veering off towards the cliff edge, dipping at the end, there! He stood, breathing hard. Sheer drop on one side and at his feet, far down, two perfect golden discs of sand divided by a bar of pale green water, just like the photo in the brochure. He'd found it. His chest was big and warm and happy. Daniel came up behind him.

'There it is – great, eh? Looks like the Caribbean. And the sun's out. Got all my cards in one shoe, boy.'

'What?'

'Y'know – got everything I want, all in one place.'

'Whatever.'

He was twelve.

'Go careful now. Very careful. Watch it.'

They did have to be careful; it was a real rabbit path, hard on the knees. Fuller couldn't be sure that this sluggish figure was truly his son; maybe he'd dart ahead the way he always had. He put out a warning arm. Sheer drop. Careful.

The surfboard was a nuisance. Glancing at the sand below, he saw people down there already. Damn. Not to worry, live and let live, hey.

'I'll let the board drop,' he called. Please let it not break, he said to himself as it slithered from his hand, pivoted on one edge and shot out of sight. Fuller turned around to take the last slope of rock backwards.

'Turn around,' he called up.

The boy would figure it out. Let him find out for himself, let him learn from something a bit tough.

All the nooks and crannies and shady spots were taken. Fuller walked the whole beach and back to where the boy had stopped, his bag dumped on the sand. Every cleft and shadow already occupied. A middle-aged couple were sauntering from one of these nooks, and something about them had the boy transfixed. Fuller looked. Not a stitch. Starkers. Perfect mahogany tans all over, their buttocks going concave as they walked, the brown flesh in shallow folds. The man had a hat on.

'Well, what is the world coming to?'

'Where are we going?' asked Daniel.

'Here's as good as anywhere, I guess.'

Fuller began to unpack the stuff. He was sure he'd brought everything: shorts, food, sun lotion, you name it, he'd got it. He flipped a ball in the boy's direction, and it rolled a way off.

'Bring your water bottle?'

Daniel looked at him.

'You didn't, did you? You forgot, didn't you? Didn't I say: bring your water bottle?'

'Well I didn't, did I?'

'We'll be short. Good job I brought mine, but we'll be short.'

'What you doing?'

'Getting the towels out.'

'That's my bag.'

'I'm getting the towels out of your bag, okay? Please Daniel, may I get the towels out?'

No reply. The boy sat down, yanked his cap further over his eyes, and looked at the sea. Fuller pulled his own shirt off and wrapped a towel tight around his waist. Still warm and happy; that sea was calling.

'Coming?'

He and his son, racing down the sand.

'Coming?'

'Maybe later.'

It would take time. One thing they had plenty of was time. He had sole custody now and the boy's mother could only have him one weekend in four, instead of the other way around; after wrangling over it for years, she'd suddenly let go of her end of the argument, like a piece of elastic. All because she was having another baby, with that jerk.

He felt curiously exposed on the sand in his shorts, out in the air. Diminished, between the two great arms of the cliff. He broke into an easy trot – yes, he was fit all right, he was the most fit parent for his son, given his secure financial status and the fact that he hadn't mucked about, like she had. She could end up living in a caravan. You'll be downsizing, he'd said to her. What do you know about anything? she mocked back. Men, always thinking size matters.

The air blew over him, made his body tight. It was good – exposed and good. Nobody was looking at him. No stopping now. Here it was, here were shallow waves like churned ice on his legs, no good stopping, get in there, throw yourself right in, aaaaaagh.

'Fantastic,' he said, towelling his head hard. 'Absolutely fantastic.' Everything glowed, shone, right into his heart. 'I'm a new man. I recommend it.'

The boy still sat, his feet buried.

'Not even going to change?' Fuller knew he should leave off, but honestly. 'The waves are pretty good. Got quite a pull. Take the board, hey—'

'I'm not using that thing. It's too small. It's for a kid.'

Fuller looked at the purple polystyrene board. It had been the best thing in the world last year; they had had just one day at the coast and Daniel had been bounced around by waves too big for him. Now he himself was too big.

'Why didn't you say? You could've said. I wouldn't have carried it all the way, would I?'

What was the point.

Daniel said, 'Can we eat?'

Of course, he was just hungry. It made you go quiet at that age when blood sugar was low. When you grow up you can go all day.

A good breakfast, you can go all day.

'Sure,' he said. 'Have a sandwich.'

The boy opened the sandwich and peeled out the meat. He didn't eat meat any more. Since when? Shrug. Since now.

Patience. Leave off.

'I'll eat it,' said Fuller. 'Waste not, want not. Go easy on the water, hey. It's all we've got.'

'I need a proper board. A long board.'

'Now, how are we going to get a long board down here?'

'They did.'

Sure enough, among the ribbon of people threading down the path, two were managing a long board between them. Fuller let out a breath through his teeth.

'Biscuit?'

The boy took the packet. 'It's too hot,' he said. 'I'm too hot down here.'

'Go in the sea. Boy, that's cold enough.'

'There's no point without a proper board.'

Fuller didn't speak. The shining glow in his chest was wearing off. 'Well, get down by the water anyway,' he said finally. 'There's a breeze there, get you cool. Don't eat all those; there'll be none for later.'

The boy sat, coiled up. Then he dropped the biscuits, rose to his feet and made off with a slow, dragging lope, turning his cap around so the peak covered his neck.

Fuller watched him. There he goes, my son, waiting to become a man. Funny to think of that. He thought about calling him back for sun lotion, but didn't. He watched him go, then set his rucksack behind his head and lay back.

Should've brought a paper.

Now who was this, right in front of him, hardly ten feet away. Getting a bit crowded. Well, it was a blazing day, all right. This lot were foreign, it was obvious, which would explain it. Different sense of personal space. Two men and three women, all plonked down as if they owned the beach.

Fuller studied them as they shed their clothes. Not down to the buff; the men wore tiny white things that looked like underwear but had small belts, so couldn't be. The women were slower to undress. They wore costumes in two pieces like old-fashioned bikinis. One was dark but otherwise they were pale in a way that northern people are rarely pale, and they all had black hair.

Fuller guessed Italian, but he wasn't sure.

He tried to hear what they were saying – not that he knew Italian, but he might recognise the sound of it. Maybe it was Romanian or Bulgarian or something; he only had a vague idea of such places. Maybe they were staff from a nearby hotel.

God, it was hot. He turned over onto his stomach and shoved his face into the towel. Then he rolled back again.

The men were small nippy types; some women go for that. Two of the women lay near the men, close, so he could tell they were couples, and that left one, on her own. She was kneeling, her arms lifted to fix up her hair, showing dark tufts in her armpits. They seemed to be teasing her. 'Son-yar!' they said. She laughed back. She wasn't especially pretty. She finished her hair and stood up, hands on hips, her belly flat and smooth. In his ex-wife's belly a new child grew, right now, at that moment.

The woman called Sonya set off towards the sea, which was now a long way off. Fuller closed his eyes.

When he opened them she was coming straight up the beach towards him, hair plastered back slick and wet off her face. Just then, the small figure of the boy crossed his line of vision, still quite far off, heading his way. Had he been gone an awful long time? It seemed so. Fuller sat up slowly, sun dizzy; he'd dozed off for a moment. He watched the boy come closer, watched him trail between the people with the sea blazing behind him.

'Hi there,' said Fuller.

'Any water left?'

He reached into the rucksack and handed over the bottle. The boy drained it and tossed it back.

'Want to swim now?' Fuller asked.

'Dunno,' said the boy. 'Might do.'

SONNY

ROB MAGNUSON SMITH

IT WAS their third summer in Cornwall when the seagull fell from the sky. Barry had been up on the ladder in the back garden, painting the window frames a more blinding white. Simon was at the cooker making his Hangover Lentils. The pair had been working with their kitchen window open to facilitate a sense of togetherness when apart.

It was hot – the garden was awash with sunlight. Down the long stretch of grass there was just the one tree, a birch in full leaf after some determined rains of spring. Barry had almost finished the second frame when there seemed a palpable break in the atmosphere, a rupture. He heard a squawk, followed by a thud. He searched the ground and there it was, a male seagull past its youth, lying in the grass.

Simon stuck his head out of the kitchen window. 'What was that?'

Barry had already climbed down. The bird opened its beak as if to greet him, but otherwise lay motionless. Up in the birch there was nothing – no companions, no explanation, just gaps in the branches where bright sunlight filtered down. High above their garden, shifting prisms in the sky had created strange portals. In their village of St Buryan, some distance from the coast, seagulls rarely appeared. There was no doubt in Barry's mind, though he favoured explanations bordering on the supernatural, that this bird had reached them after great effort, possibly breaking through from a parallel universe. By the time Simon had reached his side, he'd picked up the seagull and cradled it in his arms.

Barry had just turned fifty. He was younger than Simon by an undetermined number of years. Because he was Irish, good-looking in a bluff yet sensitive way, and he brushed his hair straight up from his forehead, everyone called him Morrissey. His chin was just the right shape for taking between thumb and forefinger – men, women and children often did so without asking. He was also a head nurse equipped with deep reservoirs of compassion. He was so naturally self-effacing, he denied that he was more appealing than anyone else. This ridiculous claim undoubtedly stemmed from his inherited Catholic guilt – a point Simon, a vocal critic of religion, made pains to repeat.

In contrast – and everybody contrasted badly with Barry – Simon was practically an old crone. Paunchy, nearly bald, cranky to his best friends and murderous to his enemies, he was the agreed brain of the pair. He spotted faults in the sublime and never hesitated to identify them. An architect originally from Hampshire, nobody knew his exact age. Wikipedia had recently put him at sixty-one, but this entry had since been removed. Yet Simon had seen pain in his past. It was the legacy of his own mistakes, his incessant sniping. Despite his critical gaze – or perhaps in reaction to it – his eyes often welled and brimmed over, forcing him to turn away.

This odd emotionality, which he explained away with venom, made Barry love him all the more. When they'd met, twelve years ago, Barry told his friends that providential forces had been at work. Meanwhile Simon – he'd seen his Morrissey and taken possession. Both believed themselves lucky, and as a consequence their relationship never foundered. They moved to Cornwall because they simply wanted to live there. It represented happiness.

It was the first seagull to visit their garden. As Barry's dropped paintbrush lay in the whitened grass, Simon stood at a distance, pale and badly hung-over, still in his dressing gown and wincing with an expression of curdled milk. Whenever Barry found a creature to care about, it threatened what he cared about – food, drink, affection.

'What are you doing? Those things carry cancer.' Barry didn't respond. He had his head lowered over the bird, and he was whispering to it. Simon released a long and exaggerated sigh. His tone softened. 'It's not dead, is it?'

'He might be in shock.' Barry turned the bird over gently and stroked the feathers on its head. The bird didn't seem to mind. It had swooned in Barry's company, like everyone else. 'No obvious injuries. Sometimes they have small heart attacks, like humans.' He met Simon's eyes with an expression of urgency. 'We've got to take it to the bird sanctuary.'

'What?' Simon tightened the belt on his dressing gown. 'Now?'

'Of course.'

'But I haven't finished my lentils.'

Barry glanced up at the trees. The prisms shifted again. New portals had opened. 'I can go by myself.'

This time Simon's sigh was genuine. He went inside to put some clothes on. Barry had dragged him to the Mousehole Bird Hospital a few times, mostly to visit a black guillemot that had made the papers. The bird had washed up on the beach coated with oil after a tanker wrecked off Penzance. He opened his wardrobe and reached for his trousers. Who knew how long this would take, following stacks of tourists on a Sunday afternoon, hunting for parking, waiting for some pious volunteer to relieve them of their burden. His lentils, his recuperative glass of cold Riesling – not to mention the evening's intimacies – all had been pushed back.

Meanwhile Barry had carried the seagull into the house. He sat on the sofa with the bird in his lap and submitted to the enthralment of holding a wild animal. Seagulls bred on every continent. They lived in noisy colonies, wary of direct human contact – yet this one rested quietly in his arms. He ran his fingers down its wings, all the way to the tips. Soon its eyes squeezed tight and its chest rose and fell less rapidly. He'd been told that, besides mammals, only birds had REM sleep. Barry tried to sense the bird's dreams. There would be an ascent into the light, up to the winds his wings could catch, before banking with a fierce screech.

Still in the bedroom, Simon found a shoebox from his second pair of dress shoes. Proud of this proof of compassion, he delivered it to Barry on the sofa.

'Alright? Stick the damn thing in here and let's go.'

'I don't know …' Barry was smoothing the bird's webbed feet. 'Maybe we shouldn't move him just yet. He's calming down. I'll run him to the bird hospital in the morning.'

'Him?'

'Most people can't tell, but they've got slightly brighter plumage than females. I think we'll call him Sonny.'

They ate lentils with Sonny on the table between them. Barry never took his eyes from the bird. He'd lined the shoebox with grass cuttings and stuffing from an old pillow. Simon's headache had finally lessened. It was the Riesling that had done it. They kept their voices low to avoid waking the bird.

'How old is he?'

'Ten, maybe twelve.'

'And how long do they live?'

'Fifteen, twenty years, on average.'

'Then he's having a midlife crisis.'

Barry put down his spoon. He reached over and dared a light stroke of the bird's head. 'Do you know – I think he came here on purpose.'

'Man is allowed his delusions.'

'Why don't you try to hold him? Later, when he wakes up?'

'Don't be daft.' Simon poured himself another glass of wine. Barry, because of his long commute the next day, would stop at one. Remarkably, he'd kept his job in Ireland. He had the longest commute of anyone they knew – a three-hour-and-fifteen-minute drive to Exeter, a one-hour flight to Dublin, followed by a thirty-minute taxi to the emergency room. He worked twelve-hour shifts for four days, slept in a bedsit, then returned to the paradise he'd earned for the rest of the week. Simon had it easy – he worked from home.

'I'll watch him the first shift. You sleep for four hours, then I'll wake you at midnight.'

Simon just stared. 'Um … how about no?'

'We have to. When Sonny wakes up, he'll be frightened. He might not remember where he is. He could try to fly.'

'And? How the hell am I going to stop him?'

'Stroking his feathers, calming him down.'

'I need to calm down. This is ridiculous.' Simon glared into the shoebox, his feelings for the animal at a new low. 'The last thing I'm going to do, mate, is stay up all night watching a bird.'

'I'll do it, then.' There wasn't any blame in Barry's voice. It was resolve.

'But you're off to Dublin tomorrow! You can't go without sleep!'

'Shh …' The seagull had stirred. He stretched his neck to a full and surprising length, then nestled back into his feathers. Barry rebuilt the grass and pillow stuffing around him. 'That's all right, Sonny.'

Simon's third sigh that day held genuine pain. He lowered his voice to a whisper. 'Why don't we just put his box outside? He wakes up, he flies away.'

'It's too cold out there at night. Think of the fox. The neighbour's cat …'

Simon didn't want to say what he thought of that. He cleared the dishes and washed up. It would have been better if they'd gone straight to Mousehole. The reasons for Barry's behaviour were clear enough. Years ago some of their friends, gay couples with money, had found surrogate mothers. These kids were getting older now, filling the social calendar with birthdays. Simon once fancied the idea of a child. He'd had a girlfriend long ago, mostly for the sake of raising a family. But Barry had always been against offspring, especially when so many others needed care. Now that he'd reached fifty, he'd sacrificed this window of opportunity, and the seagull was generating regret.

Simon took the rest of the bottle to bed. He had plenty of regrets of his own – but at least his were known to him. He didn't suffer from delusions. He tried to read himself to sleep, but he kept thinking of the advancing minutes before his watch. Once, he got up and crept into the sitting room. The television was on. Barry was still on the sofa, staring into the shoebox, whispering words only the seagull could hear.

At midnight, Simon was shaken awake. His eyes felt swollen and he could barely see. Barry stood over the bed with the gall to smile. 'Your turn.'

'Come on. Don't make me …'

'You don't have to. If you'd rather sleep.'

'Oh, God. Oh, all right.'

'You sure?'

'No.' Simon groaned and reached for his book. 'For the love of vermin …'

'Wake me if there's a problem. Okay?'

Simon nodded. A little later he was on the sofa in his dressing gown and slippers, a pot of coffee on the side table. In the bedroom he could hear Barry snoring.

The minutes crept by. He read his book, but he found himself increasingly drawn to the shoebox and the seagull. They'd never had pets. He had to admit it was oddly comforting, sharing an evening with a sleeping animal. At one point Sonny turned over. Stretching out his neck, he stared straight at Simon with an unblinking eye.

Maybe he was still hung-over, maybe it was fatigue. But looking into the eye of a seagull was unnerving. It was like peering over a cliff, or into a moving river. How in the world had these birds survived? The ancient volcanoes had spewed out lava. The continents had risen and broken apart, and for all the millions of years the earth was capable of supporting life, through the meteors and ice ages, seagulls had held on. Now they were landing in back gardens, sharing sofas with humans in Cornwall. Maybe Sonny had known what he was doing. Maybe he'd seen Barry on the ladder and was smart enough to know he'd be safe.

Simon nodded off, then pushed through the limits of his exhaustion. There was no choice but to place a value to this effort, to convince himself he was doing something right. He put on a film, drank more coffee. He couldn't believe Barry hadn't prepared anything for the bird to eat in case it woke up hungry. So he hurried into the kitchen, tore pieces of chicken from yesterday's roast and added potatoes. He chewed the food up and left it in a mash on a plate. He'd never liked seagulls – their scavenging disgusted him – but he'd be damned if the bird expired on his watch.

In the middle of the night something brought his memories back, all the way to childhood – sitting on his dad's shoulders, eating monkey nuts. Both parents were gone now. He started to feel sorry for himself, and for the small life man had. He'd wanted to be an architect so that he wouldn't be smaller still. He'd designed over forty buildings, but never could he create the sensation of looking into that unblinking eye.

Suddenly the bird was sitting up, trying to stand. Its little legs buckled and gave way. It tilted its head, opened its beak and made a faint, pathetic cry.

Simon listened for a sound from the bedroom. Barry was still snoring. 'Morning, Sonny! You hungry?'

The bird just stared. Simon extended the plate of mashed chicken and potatoes. Seagulls snatched ice cream cones from grown men in Newquay. This one couldn't get his head out of a shoebox.

He put the plate down and tossed a bit of chicken on the grass. Sonny moved his beak over, made a gurgling sound, then snapped it up. Simon had respect for any bird that ate bird. He flung bits of food into the box until the plate was finished. Sonny blinked at him with his visible eye, tucked his beak into his chest feathers and went back to sleep.

Simon smiled. Throughout the night he stared into the shoebox, willing the bird to get better.

At five in the morning, Barry appeared at the sofa. Sonny looked much more alert. He was sitting up in the shoebox and nibbling at the stuffing from the pillow.

'You mean he ate the whole plate of food?'

'Every bit.'

'How did you know to mash it up?'

'That's what they do, isn't it? The parents?'

'You've given him strength, Simon. Did he try to stand?'

'Once. It didn't work, though – he sat right back down.'

Barry put his hand into the box. Sonny didn't flinch as he stroked his head. It struck him as troubling. 'He should have tried to fly, I should think. He looks healthier, but I'm worried. I'll drop him at the hospital on the way to work.'

'No, you go on.' Simon looked at the seagull. Sonny was watching them, back and forth, like a spectator at a tennis match. 'I can take him in later.'

'What if something goes wrong?'

'I've watched him all night, haven't I? Go on. Don't miss your flight.'

'Let's go together. I mean, in separate cars. After we drop him at the hospital, I'll carry on to Exeter.'

'Who gets to take Sonny?'

In the end, they drove to Mousehole in Barry's car, with Simon holding the seagull in his lap. He said he could do with the walk home.

The bird hospital stood on a steep cliff above the village. It had been started by two sisters, long since dead. It was dawn and still a while before opening hours. Barry rang the emergency number, and soon a woman appeared on foot. 'What have you got?' She noticed Barry and stared. 'Wow. Anyone ever told you that you look like Morrissey?'

'Male seagull. Approximately ten.' Simon held out the shoebox. He explained how Sonny had dropped from the sky, how he'd eaten both chicken and potatoes.

'Great,' she said. 'We'll take care of him.'

'Can we visit?'

The woman hadn't stopped staring at Barry. 'We're open every day.'

It wasn't until the following week, after Barry was back from Dublin, that they returned. They found parking in Mousehole and walked up the steep road to the bird hospital. The gate was open. Simon groaned at the number of steps before them. 'I never should have fallen for a Catholic.'

Barry could tell he'd been drinking more heavily, as he typically did when left alone. He'd been upset about losing Sonny, and about getting attached in such a short period of time. They'd spoken about it on the phone while Barry was away. Barry had been forced to lie. He'd said there was no question that Simon had saved a life. He said the bird would remember.

They went up the crumbling steps to the entrance. A waiting room held musty magazines, bird calendars and donation boxes. The aviary came into view – outdoor enclosures of concrete floors and wire fencing. Most of the enclosures were empty. A member of staff was scattering seed for a one-legged rook.

'Excuse me,' Simon called. 'We brought in a seagull a few days ago?'

'Up on the next level,' she said.

They walked up the second flight of steps. Along the walls were frescoes, icons of saints, statues of Francis of Assisi embedded in the rock. The smell of the sea wafted through the mist. At the top, they reached the seagull enclosure. It was a bit crowded.

'Is that him?'

'No. That one, there.'

'Or the one with the extra red on his beak?'

'Could be …'

Together, they faced the birds. There must have been thirty of them. Some were sitting on the concrete, others standing.

Barry raised his voice. 'Sonny?'

Simon clapped his hands. 'Here, Sonny!'

The seagulls turned their heads in unison. Simon and Barry stood at the cage, waiting for any sign of recognition. For what seemed the longest time, the seagulls kept watching them as if they were the only humans left.

THE SUPERPOWER

SARAH PERRY

BY SOME miracle, Stanley and May shared the same superpower. They didn't give it much attention. Sometimes they forgot about it altogether. That was the trick, not going on about it. It underpinned their marriage and kept them on the level, during the good times and the bad. What were the odds of two people having the same superpower, their paths crossing and then marrying each other?

Fergus Treves, a small, terrier-like journalist with big ambitions, had discovered them quite by chance. On his day off, he'd driven out to a favourite spot tucked away on the Tamar, where swallows and salmon skim the surface of the water for insects. Time slowed down as he drove over the bridge into Cornwall. The hum of a tractor comforted him. He watched a flock of newly shorn sheep nuzzling the ground for grass. And then on a bend in the road, out of the corner of his eye he glimpsed a sign for free-range eggs. It was written in white chalk on a heavy slab of slate beside a bumpy farm track. In his rear-view mirror, he watched the entrance of the lane disappear behind him. A curtain of dust spread and settled, as his car negotiated the stony dry pits and potholes that would have been muddy puddles a few weeks earlier.

He bought a bunch of the bluest cornflowers he'd ever seen, as well as half a dozen eggs. And somehow he ended up having a cup of tea with Stanley and May, chatting about this and that on a wooden form outside the back door of the farmhouse. Fergus asked some questions about farming, not really interested in the answers, just wanting to postpone his eventual departure.

Stanley sucked on his pipe, then tapped it against the stone wall to unblock the dregs of tobacco, refilled and relit it again, drawing in so deeply the embers glowed.

'The point is, in farming, you're working with living things – a grain of corn, a flower – they're all living and if you look after them, they'll produce.'

May backed up Stanley's reflections. 'I have my hens. I sell my hens' eggs and have enough to pay the groceries from that money. There you are. We love our animals.'

It was only after he'd left the dusty lane that Fergus noticed he felt very different. It was something he couldn't put his finger on, but his curiosity was aroused. He remembered one thing Stanley and May had said, about being the subject of a research study conducted at the university. Once Fergus caught the scent of a story, he didn't let up.

May wished she'd had her hair washed and set a few days earlier. She patted the bottom of her hairdo with the palm of her hand, with the hope of finding an inner bounce in her follicles, but her hair remained stiff and unyielding on the top of her head. By tomorrow, it would have dropped and softened and looked less starchy. Never mind.

They'd been reluctant to take part in the television interview. The taxi and three-course meal had won them over. They didn't have to drive anywhere and it was a day off from cooking for May.

'In my series of interviews we have met some remarkable people, but these two people are by far the most extraordinary. I would like to introduce you to Stanley and May, the last two people on earth with what scientists have only recently identified as a superpower. It was thought this superpower vanished with the death of Janet Hodge in 2011, so we are incredibly excited to find it still exists and lives on in Stanley and May. So, May, can I talk to you first?' Fergus said. 'When did you first know you had this superpower?'

May thought it had been handed down to her, so it wasn't something she felt she could take credit for. She didn't like the fuss. 'I think I was more like my mother. The stamina and work. I don't know any other really.' She sat back, having said her bit.

Fergus growled internally; he realised May was a woman of few words. It would be like drawing blood from a stone. He turned and wagged his finger at Stanley. 'Right, ah, and what about you Stanley? What can you tell us about the origins of your superpower?'

Stanley was waiting for his turn. Although a little nervous, he felt he had something important to say. He caught sight of himself in the camera directly in front of him. His head looked brown and smooth like a hazelnut. Not bad for a man of seventy-six years, he thought to himself. 'I think it stems back to my army career. I had to stand on my own two feet. In the army you have to stand on your own two feet. You've got to learn to do your ironing …'

'He's not ironed since we got married,' May interjected quietly, with a trace of humour. The audience tittered.

'But I had to learn, you see. Ironing in the army, you've got to iron to perfection. You've got to have creases everywhere, in your trousers and shirts. I could iron to perfection if I wanted to.'

'I always thought he would be a good husband because he was good to his mother. When they're good to their mother, they're usually good to their wife. His mother thought the world of him.'

Fergus shifted in his seat. He sensed Stanley and May were leading him down a rabbit hole. He'd have to round them up. 'So, it could be genes, it could be the army training, or it could be something else altogether.'

'But there again, Mam, when we moved into the farm, we weren't under the same pressure. That's the answer to it!'

May wished Stanley wouldn't refer to her as Mam in front of people. But she was many things to him.

Fergus's ears pricked. There was some fidgeting in the auditorium that he needed to get on top of. He flashed his teeth and turned to the audience. 'I'd like to introduce Dr Sheila Scott, from the School of Positive Psychology at the University of West Britain. Dr Scott, can you shed some light on this superpower and explain to us why Stanley and May are the only two people left with it?'

As Dr Scott took a deep breath, she wondered how in hell she was going to condense a lifetime's work into a sound bite. 'As you know, we have been classifying human strengths and virtues for the last fifty years. In our international research project we have listed forty-two character strengths in total. Then five years ago, we noticed certain strengths were becoming increasingly difficult to identify in populations right across the world. Indeed, we started talking about the disappearance and, in some cases, the absolute extinction of specific strengths in humankind. Because of their rarity we started to refer to these strengths as "superpowers".

'Our understanding of these superpowers is very limited. We have lost the ability to recognise them. Our brains, despite or because of their complexity, don't perceive them any more. Even when we do succeed in isolating them, we find them extremely difficult to capture – it's hard to find the words; they elude us. Many scientists have lost their minds over this.'

May felt sorry for the doctor's predicament. She meant no harm in having this superpower, but it seemed to be upsetting these very educated people.

'Stanley and May are anomalies, outliers,' Dr Scott continued, getting into her stride. 'They are statistically and clinically significant. They have completed numerous standardised psychological measures, but the School has been mystified by one consistent finding: Stanley and May cannot be categorised.'

May caught Fergus's eye and raised her hand a little just to let him know there was something she wanted to say. 'I'd describe myself as very contented and easy-going. And, ah, not one who wants everything. Just an ordinary farmer's wife. I don't wish for a lot, but wish everyone had success in their lives and was happy.' She hoped that would help a little, but couldn't be sure it was enough.

Fergus noticed a calmness slowly creep over his body as he listened to Stanley and May. The room went quiet. He thought to himself, If this is all I'm remembered for, this interview, then I'll be happy. And then it struck him. Perhaps this was what contentment felt like. He was about to leap out of his chair and announce, 'I've got the superpower too! I have contentment!' But he hesitated and in that split second he had a worrying thought. How would he keep hold of it? And just like that, the superpower disappeared, like a strip of sunlight on wooden floorboards, extinguished by a small silent cloud passing over the sun.

May remembered there were two shop-bought chocolate éclairs in the fridge back home, filled with fresh cream. They'd go off if they weren't eaten today.

'Let's forget about the three-course meal, Stan,' she whispered under her breath. 'We can't eat like we used to. There's a bit of ham in the fridge and a couple of chocolate éclairs. You like them.'

Although he didn't have much of a sweet tooth, Stanley was relieved May had made the first move. 'Let's leave them to it.' He took the opportunity to round things off. 'Well, a favourite saying of mine is, "Not everything that counts can be counted, and not everything that can be counted counts." Albert Einstein said that, you know, and you might find that a good bit of advice. I have.'

THE HAUNTING
OF BODMIN JAIL

ANASTASIA
GAMMON

SCREAMS CUT across the sound of glass shattering. Shards flew everywhere and feet leapt backwards, away from the glass and, presumably, the spirit who had knocked over the wooden table and sent it flying in the first place.

'It's okay,' Jane said to the guests, all huddled in groups around the cold, dark room. Jane held her hands out and kept her voice level, calm, as she carefully tiptoed around the broken pieces of glass and towards the door. 'I think perhaps we might have out-stayed our welcome.' She smiled and a few of the guests let out small, uncertain laughs, fingers unclenching ever so slightly from the arms of the friends beside them. 'Now is probably a good time for us to call it a night anyway.'

Under the modern, fluorescent lights of the cloakroom, fright quickly turned to relief and excitement at having had a real paranormal experience. Jane saw the guests safely back to their cars, graciously accepted their praise for her work, and, only once the very last one had driven away from the jail, returned to pick up the wooden table and place it carefully back on the hidden spring mechanism she stood on every night to tip it over and send the glass flying. She swept up the shards with the dustpan and brush from the cleaning cupboard, turned off the silent fans that sent periodic bursts of cold air out of two of the cells on the second floor, and retrieved her phone from the hidden speaker on the third floor where it had been playing the sounds of whispers and jangling chains earlier in the evening.

It was almost 6 a.m. before Jane was ready to leave. She grabbed her things from the staffroom, thinking already of her soft bed in her warm flat. When she finally stepped out of the jail's front door, a figure was waiting for her on the other side of the empty car park. The figure waved and Jane's teeth ground together. Ed.

'What are you doing here?' Jane asked, voice hushed, as she hurried across the car park.

'I wanted to surprise you.' Ed grinned.

'Well, you surprised me. Now let's go.' Jane tried to get past but Ed took a step in the other direction, back towards the jail.

'How was work?' he asked, still smiling, still slowly backing further in the opposite direction to where Jane wanted to be.

'It was perfect,' Jane said. 'Peaceful. Not a single ghost anywhere in sight.'

'Sounds boring,' Ed teased.

'No, it was very exciting, and I'll tell you all about it on the way home.' Jane turned halfway towards the road again.

'Or you could show me …'

'No.'

'Oh, come on. I'm here now.' Before Jane could say another word in argument, Ed had skipped across the car park and straight through the solid wooden door of the jail.

Jane groaned. She looked out at the road and thought about leaving anyway. She could just go home. Ed would probably get bored after a few minutes and come after her. She might be in bed already before he even realised she wasn't coming. There was nothing stopping her from just leaving him there.

Ed was waiting on the other side of the door when Jane opened it, a self-satisfied smile on his face.

'What if someone comes in and sees me talking to you?' Jane demanded in a whisper.

'Isn't talking to ghosts literally your job?' Ed asked, whispering himself even though no one else could hear him. Jane paused. She hated it when Ed was right.

'You're the worst,' Jane snapped.

Ed silently slapped his hand on his chest, right where his heart would have been if he still had one. His chest still moved as though he did; it was eerie when Jane thought about it for too long. 'You wound me, Jane. Tell me you don't mean it.'

'I won't.'

'All right, then.' Ed's hand fell back to his side. 'Give me the ghost tour to make it up to me.'

Ed straightened his tattered brown jacket, smoothing it unnecessarily with his fingers. Jane spent a lot of time looking at Ed's hands. He could pick things up when he wanted to. He could pass his hands through walls as though they were made of nothing and he could use them to lift the sofa for Jane when she vacuumed. She had never spent enough time with a ghost before Ed to notice things like that. Sometimes she made him pick things up and then pass a hand through them in the same minute, just to see him do it.

Working nights as the jail's resident medium meant she didn't have a whole lot of other things to occupy her time.

'Fine.' Ed grinned widely again but Jane held up a hand to stop him before he could get too excited. 'I'll show you around but I'm not doing the whole tour. I will not commune with imaginary ghosts in front of you.'

Ed pretended to consider this for a moment, pallid lips pursed and dark eyes narrowed. 'Okay. Let's go.' Ed held his arm out, elbow crooked, as though he expected Jane to entwine her own arm with his and lead him away.

Jane shoved her hands into the pockets of her jeans. 'This way.'

Jane had only been working at the jail for a few months. It had been a tip from a cousin with similar abilities; the most haunted place in Great Britain wasn't actually haunted at all and they were looking for someone new to pretend that it was. Jane's cousin had gone for an interview first, really believing that she might be able to use the job to help some poor abandoned souls find peace. When she had realised there weren't any poor abandoned souls to be found, she had recommended Jane immediately.

It had seemed too good to be true for Jane. She had no interest in helping abandoned souls if she could avoid it, but she certainly had enough experience to convince people that that was exactly what she did every night. And if they wanted to pay her then who was she to complain? She had even managed to find a small house for rent, fully furnished, just a twenty-minute walk from the jail; most importantly, it had been built only eleven years ago. The chances of anyone having died in it were so slim Jane had signed the lease without even visiting it in person.

So Jane had only had herself to blame when she showed up with all of her belongings and found Ed perched on the arm of the sofa. In her shock, Jane had screamed and dropped a box of books on her foot. In his, Ed had fallen straight through the sofa and the floor beneath it.

Now, Ed was standing in front of one of the mannequins in the jail's historical exhibition, his nose two inches away from its wax face.

'These things are creepy.' This particular mannequin had its hands tied behind its back, waiting forever for another mannequin to put its head through a noose. Jane had to agree with Ed. The mannequins all had these buggy eyes that followed you around the room. She couldn't really blame anyone for believing the place was haunted with those things everywhere you looked. 'So, what do you do in here then?' Ed asked, slipping through the wooden gate that was supposed to keep people away from the exhibition.

Jane gestured vaguely down the hall in the direction of the cells with the hidden fans. 'Blast them with cold air and keep them talking so they don't hear the fans.' Ed started walking towards the cells in question, backwards so that he could still look at Jane while she explained. Jane followed. 'I tell them about prisoners who were kept in these cells and their imaginations fill in the blanks.'

'What prisoners?' Ed asked.

Jane shrugged. 'I make them up. Men who killed their wives, women wrongly accused, children born in the cells who died of starvation. I try to figure out what ghost they want and give it to them.' The lot who had just left had been very pleased with their lady serial killer.

Ed stopped suddenly. So did Jane. 'What ghost would you make up for me?' he asked, smirking again.

'A really annoying one.'

'More annoying than me?'

'My imagination isn't that good.'

Ed's laugh was like static on Jane's skin.

They kept going, Ed asking questions about what Jane did here, and what she told the guests here, only coming to a stop again when they reached one of the more popular exhibits. This time the mannequin was a young woman with long brunette hair, endlessly about to drop one child down a well, another clinging to her skirts.

'Selina Wadge. She was a real prisoner.'

'I know.' Ed was still, his voice quiet. 'I remember.'

They had never talked about Ed's life, or how he died, or how he came to be haunting a house built at least one hundred years too late for him to have ever lived in it. From his tattered jacket and patched-up trousers, Jane had guessed that he had probably been alive in the late nineteenth century, and she knew that ghosts could haunt people instead of places, sometimes even families down the generations, and get stuck when the last person died. She had never asked if that was what had happened to Ed though. For some reason, with him, it didn't seem polite.

'During the day they have a film they project,' Jane said instead, 'with an actress playing her.' Ed nodded but Jane didn't think he was really listening. 'Did you know her?' she asked, her voice almost a whisper.

'No.' Ed smiled, and shot her a sidelong look as if to say that not everyone from the nineteenth century knew each other. 'I just remember hearing about it.'

'People think they can feel her on the third and fourth floors but there's nothing there. It's just this place.'

Ed turned away from the exhibit. He opened his mouth as if to say something but his eyes passed over Jane to a spot somewhere behind her. 'Are you sure about that?' he asked.

Jane felt something drop in the pit of her stomach. The room had gone cold. Or maybe that was just the dread building up, freezing her from the inside. Slowly, she turned around. At the other end of the hallway stood a young woman in a long dress, faintly glowing and staring, not at Jane, but at Ed.

Jane swore under her breath. The woman's dark eyes flickered to Jane's face. The two of them looked at each other across the hallway for barely a moment. Then the woman turned and fled, her skirt billowing behind her.

Jane swore louder this time. 'This is your fault,' she said, pointing a finger at Ed.

Ed's mouth fell open. 'How is it my fault?'

'You attracted her here with your … ghost energy.'

'My ghost energy?'

'Yes.'

'Isn't it more likely that she's been here for a long time, hiding, waiting for someone who could help her, and seeing you interact with a real spirit has encouraged her to show herself to you?'

'Either way, it's your fault.' This was exactly why Jane hadn't wanted Ed in the jail in the first place. She knew something like this would happen.

Jane was so angry she didn't even wait to see if Ed was following before she took off after the woman. Of course, by the time she reached the end of the hallway, there was no longer any trace of the new ghost.

'She could be anywhere.'

As if on cue, Jane heard a bang from upstairs, so loud it made her jump. Dust rained down from the ceiling above. She took the stairs two at a time.

'What are you going to do?' Ed asked, right behind her.

'I'm going to get rid of her.'

They found the woman in front of one of the cells on the fourth floor. The wooden gate that should have been in the doorway of the cell was lying on the floor, in pieces, next to the glowing figure. She was staring into the small room, standing perfectly still. The air was so cold Jane could see her breath forming clouds in front of her.

'Why is she glowing?' Ed whispered. 'I don't glow.' He was standing so close that Jane almost thought she could feel his breath on the back of her neck.

'She's a different kind of ghost.'

'What kind?'

The woman turned slowly. Her dress barely moved. Unlike Ed, she floated above the ground.

'Tricky,' Jane answered.

The woman was staring at them now, her expression entirely unreadable. A chill went down Jane's spine. It had been a long time since she'd done this.

'Selina?' she asked, taking a single step towards the woman. The woman tilted her head to the side, her unblinking eyes still fixed on Jane. Jane took the woman's stillness as a sign that it was okay to keep moving slowly towards her.

'I don't think it's her,' Ed said. 'She looks too young.' Now that they were closer, Jane could see that he was right. The woman she had mistaken for Selina Wadge was barely a woman at all. She had a soft, round face, and her dark eyes were wide and curious. She didn't look any older than fourteen.

'What's your name?' Jane asked. The girl's frowning mouth stayed shut. 'I'm Jane and this is Ed.' Jane stopped halfway down the hallway, not wanting to go any further until she was sure the girl wouldn't rip off any more gates or flee again. 'I can help you. Will you tell me your name?'

'I don't remember it,' the girl said. Her voice was deeper than Jane had expected – husky, like the jazz singers Jane's grandmother had loved.

'Okay.' If this girl truly didn't remember who she was, then this was going to be even trickier than Jane had thought. 'Do you know where you are?'

'I've been away.' The girl switched her gaze to Ed. 'You're dead too.'

'Oh. Yes. I am.' Ed stepped out from behind Jane. The girl mirrored the movement, lifting her own feet a little too high, like a child just learning to walk.

'Is she helping you?' the girl asked, her wide eyes focused on Ed's face again, rather than his feet.

Ed looked at Jane, puffed out his cheeks, and thought about his answer. 'Yes,' he said at last. 'In a way.'

Jane didn't have time for this ghostly bonding. The sky was already starting to lighten outside the jail's small windows and she had to get rid of this girl before anyone else arrived. She wanted to get home before someone found that broken gate and started asking questions.

'Do you know why you're here?' Jane asked.

'No. I don't know any of this. Why do you keep asking me questions?' The girl's frown deepened, her eyebrows lowered. Jane took a step back.

'I want to help you move on from here.'

'To where?'

'To the next place.' That was what Jane's grandmother had always said. That was what she had taught her granddaughters to say. None of it ever sounded quite right coming out of Jane's mouth.

'I don't want to go anywhere.' The glow around the girl started to intensify, and her mouth began to twist further down. Jane fell to the floor instinctively, her knees crashing painfully on the concrete. She curled up into a ball and pressed her hands over her ears just in time.

The girl let out a deafening, high-pitched scream and for the second time that night Jane heard the sound of glass smashing, but this time she was pretty sure it was a window or two.

Jane waited until she was certain that the ghost was quite finished before uncurling from her defensive ball. Ed was still standing in exactly the same place, but the girl was gone.

'What was that?' Ed asked, still staring at the spot where the other ghost had been.

'A poltergeist.' Jane brushed the dust from her knees and swore again. 'I shouldn't have asked her all those questions. I've just made it worse.'

'You barely spoke to her,' Ed argued. 'She was a brat.'

Jane looked down at her watch. She only had an hour and a half until the jail opened for visitors. There was no way she could leave a ghost that angry and confused wandering around in a place that would soon be full of families and tourists. The girl had already broken one gate and at least one window, and Jane knew that would barely be the start. But if the girl couldn't even remember her own name then Jane didn't stand a chance of finding out how to move her on before opening time.

'So,' Ed asked, 'what now?'

'There's one other thing I could try.' It was something her grand-mother had shown her how to do, only in extreme circumstances. It was incredibly risky and Jane had never done it on her own before but soon people would start to flood in. 'I need you to get me a few things.'

It didn't take Ed long to get everything that Jane needed. Speed was one of the perks of being dead. You didn't have to worry about bumping into anything. Jane sat on the floor, her legs crossed, with the items Ed had retrieved spread out in front of her. There was a plastic bottle filled with holy water taken from the nearest church, a small pile of dirt with a single butter-yellow dandelion poking out of it, two candles stolen from a shop in town, and a human thigh bone, which Ed would return to the grave he had borrowed it from as soon as they were finished. He wasn't particularly happy about that one and Jane had to admit she didn't much like it either, but her grandmother had always used a human bone and Jane wasn't sure it would work with one from any other animal.

'So what exactly are you doing?' Ed asked. He was standing a little way away, watching Jane unscrew the blue plastic cap of the holy water.

'I'm going to open a door.'

'To heaven?'

'To wherever people go when they aren't here any more. Then either our new friend is going to walk through it willingly or I will push her.' Jane checked her watch. She looked up at Ed. He was twisting the ends of his jacket in his hands, his lips a thin line. He was nervous. It made Jane feel a little better to know she wasn't the only one.

Jane had offered to help Ed move on just once, on the first day they met. Well, more like she had begged him to let her help, so she could have back the quiet, ghostless existence she wanted. He had declined. He had said he didn't know why he was still there but he didn't mind it. He was sure he would move on one day, when he was ready, and in the meantime, he promised not to be any trouble. That was the last time they had talked about it. Perhaps she should have offered again since then, but Jane had grown so used to Ed being around that not having him there had become unthinkable.

She thought about telling him that once the door was open he would only have to walk through it. She thought about telling him that he should leave now and wait for her at home to be safe. In the end, she simply closed her eyes, took a deep breath, and lit the candles.

The door opened with a sound like stone being torn in two. All the air seemed to rush from the room and a different air swept back in, hotter and colder all at once. Jane's heart beat in her throat. She had done it. She could feel it on her skin, a charge one thousand times more powerful than even Ed's laugh, and the smell of dust and fire that she remembered so well from watching her grandmother do this many years ago.

She never thought she would be able to do it alone.

Jane blinked and the poltergeist was in front of her, looking into the door. She could feel it too. It was so powerful it had drawn her to it. Jane didn't dare look at Ed. She was about to say something to the girl, to start a speech about how she simply had to go through the door to be free, or something like that anyway, but before Jane could get the words out, someone stepped out of the door.

Then another someone.

Before Jane knew it, she was surrounded by dozens of various, confused ghosts.

'Is this supposed to happen?' Ed whispered, close to Jane's ear. She was so shocked that she hadn't even noticed him moving nearer.

'No,' Jane squeaked. She didn't know what to do. This had never happened when her grandmother did it. She cleared her throat. 'Excuse me.' Her words were drowned out by the sound of ghosts chatting to one another. They didn't even seem to notice her sitting there.

Sunlight was streaming through the windows now, thick bands of it illuminating every single ghost who wasn't supposed to be there.

'Help,' Jane pleaded, turning her head so fast that her nose passed through Ed's. He nodded and took a deep, useless breath, before standing up.

'Hello,' Ed said, loud enough for everyone to hear. 'Sorry to interrupt,' he continued as the chatting started to die down. 'But I'm afraid you've all made a wrong turn, so if you wouldn't mind all just heading back through that door –'

'Hang on,' a man in a cloth cap with only one visible tooth lisped. 'Who are you?'

'My name is Edward but that's really not important. If you could all just go on straight through that door there.'

'Maybe we don't want to.' A woman with short, straight hair turned her nose up at the door.

'Yeah, maybe we want to have a bit of fun,' the first man agreed.

'It's been a long time since we got to see the real world.' The ghosts all started talking over each other again in agreement.

Jane was panicking. Her heart was beating so fast she was sure it would give out at any moment. She couldn't even get in enough of the dusty air to breathe.

'You have to go back,' she said, her voice barely above a whisper.

'Says who?' A woman with long, dark hair stepped forward from the crowd and looked straight into Jane's eyes. Jane knew who she was instantly. Her eyes were less buggy but apart from that, miraculously, she didn't look so very different from her mannequin.

There were general noises of agreement from the rest of the ghosts. The girl with no name smirked.

'You don't want to be out here,' Ed said. He flung an arm around a man with one leg. 'Trust me. I've been stuck out here for over a hundred years now. It's torture. Have you ever heard of reality TV?'

'What's TV?' the woman with the short hair asked.

'What's TV?' Ed laughed. 'Oh, I can't tell you how much I wish I didn't know what TV was. And that's not even the worst of it. They all have these little computers in their pockets that tell them what to do and how to think and they take them everywhere. Jane, show them your little computer.' Jane fumbled to get her phone out of her pocket and hold it up for the ghosts to see. 'She never leaves it alone. It's sad, really.'

Selina Wadge was suddenly a breath away from Jane, her long hair swinging forward as she peered down at Jane's phone. 'What's a computer?' she asked.

'Careful,' Ed warned. 'Don't get too close. You might get addicted like she is.' Selina jumped back and a few of the other ghosts seemed to move a little closer to the door. 'Honestly, it's so boring out here these days. All they ever do is stare at those things. Isn't that right, Jane?' Jane nodded. Ed started to guide the man with one leg back towards the door. 'This isn't the place for us. Not any more. Now, let's get you all back where you're supposed to be before Big Brother finds us.'

'Who's that?' the girl with no name asked as Ed shepherded her through.

'You don't want to know,' he said seriously.

Selina Wadge was the last ghost to go back. For a moment that felt altogether too long for Jane, Selina stood on the threshold, looking around at the old stone walls of the jail. Then, at last, she stepped through. They were all gone. Except Ed.

Jane didn't feel relieved. She felt numb. Empty.

'Well?' Ed said. 'Close it before any more get through for God's sake.'

Jane swallowed her heart. 'I might not be able to open it again,' she said softly. 'This might be your only chance.'

'Oh.' Ed looked back over his shoulder. Standing there, in front of the door, he had a sort of glow around him, like the girl with no name had had. In a flash Jane saw Ed walking through, and imagined herself going back to the empty house, alone, never hearing him laugh again. Jane's hands clenched, a vain attempt to hold herself together.

Ed turned back to her, a small smile on his pale face. He stepped away from the door, towards Jane, and the glow faded. 'I'll live,' he said, with a shrug.

'No, Ed, you should go. You should be at peace.' Another one of her grandmother's lines that felt heavy on Jane's tongue.

'Do you want me to go?' Ed asked. The smile had fallen from his face and the pain Jane saw there instead was too much. Her vision blurred with tears.

'Of course not.' Jane's voice cracked. 'But you shouldn't be stuck here.'

'I want to be stuck here,' Ed insisted, sounding desperate now. 'Jane. Close the door.' Jane knew she could push him through it. She had seen her grandmother do it countless times. All she had to do was reach out and give a little push. She didn't even have to touch him.

It would be for the best. Ed could be where he was supposed to be. Jane could give him the peace he deserved.

Jane blew out the candles. The door closed, all the air rushed back into the room, and Ed still stood in front of her.

'You were going to push me.'

Jane wiped the tears from her eyes. 'No, I wasn't,' she answered truthfully.

'I'll go when I'm good and ready,' Ed told her, shoving his hands into the pockets of his jacket. 'Don't try anything like that again.'

'Sorry,' Jane said. She was more exhausted than she had ever been in her life. Her bones felt tired.

'I'm sorry I attracted a poltergeist to your place of work with my ghost energy,' Ed replied. Jane let out a noise that was somewhere between a laugh and a sob. Ed smiled.

'Good. Now that's sorted …' Ed reached out a hand towards Jane. It was solid in her grip and not at all cold. 'Let's go home.'

THE SIREN OF TREEN

EMMA STAUGHTON

Now the Sirens have a still more fatal weapon than their song, namely their silence. And though admittedly such a thing never happened, it is still conceivable that someone might possibly have escaped from their singing; but from their silence certainly never.

Franz Kafka, from The Silence of the Sirens, 1917

MORWENNA

AN EVENING mist has fallen away from the moon, slipped sideways like a veil from her cuttlebone face. I watch as heaven's brittlestars pierce the night-blue sky above Cape Cornwall and moonlight adjusts the scene to ghostly day. Except it isn't day, but some otherworldly place where cattle stand, motionless zinc sculptures in grey-green fields, and the tin roofs of the milking shed gleam, corrugated slabs of silver in the yard.

On nights like these I wonder if you are watching her too, the moon. This luminous Neptune's orb, which pushes and pulls at the edges of the ocean and squeezes my head until I'm wild. Even the cat is wild, tonight. She's vying for a fight amongst the bedcovers, flexing hooked talons from soft mittens and whipping a venomous tail. My coaxing hand is too slow, and she has me and draws blood. I push her away and suck at the red scratch oozing from the back of my hand. I wish I could sleep through this madness, but I don't sleep much these days.

I talk to you instead.

She's come back, you know. The child. Blew in with a February fog. Of course you know. Maybe you sent her back to remind me? Did you think I could forget? There are some things a woman never forgets. She thinks I don't know – she has an Irish accent and has changed her name to Clodagh – but I'd know your daughter anywhere. To see her and Matthew together: the hair, the height, the eyes, they could be twins. Tell me, what should I do?

The cursor blinks. I wait. Nothing.

Some days when I type a message I can hear you speak. Perhaps I'm imagining it? Second-guessing a response, remembering the uncomplicated logic of your replies and the comforting timbre of your voice. The cat reappears on the bed and makes a point of ignoring me. She turns her tortoiseshell back and begins to groom with a rasping tongue, and I catch the rancid scent of fish on her breath. We tolerate each other for a while, and then I push her off the bed and resume typing.

There is too much time to think when you cannot speak. Seconds seem like hours and hours like days. I find myself remembering your face. Like an Atlantic wave on a cold spring day, the sight of your face whipped my breath away, that first day on the beach at Sennen. We belonged, you and I, like the sea horses below the waves and the bracken and furze up on the moor, tangled together for life. But I never expected this.

I must have dropped off to sleep at dawn, because I can hear Matthew coming in from milking. The thud of the kitchen door below, the metallic scrape and clank of the kettle being moved across the range from warming plate to hot plate. The little squeal of the hot plate lid as he raises it. The rattle of dog biscuits as they hit three stainless steel bowls, destined for the collies in the yard. There is a reassuring sequence to the percussion of morning sounds.

I shift arthritic limbs and prop myself up against the pillows to stare out across the farmyard. Gone is the ghostly moonlit scene, replaced by the detritus of farming life. A moss-tinged rusty landscape of tin roofs, the Delabole slates long gone (sold for cash decades back), decomposing tractor parts, hens pecking for bugs and grain amongst last year's mouldy straw bales, a pile of sheep hurdles, gates, galvanised troughs and the rusting remains of my brother's Massey Ferguson tractor. Beyond, the clouds, the sky, the granite-edged fields, the telegraph poles … everything seems tilted towards the ocean, which flickers – a flatlined shallow cup of blue on the horizon.

Matthew's here. I try to smile and fail as he knocks, enters and walks across the room with a cup of tea. He says good morning and stoops to kiss my misshapen cheek, slopping tea into the saucer. We dance around the spillage for a while, he puts the cup down on the bedside chest, I tug a tissue from a box and dab, he lifts the cup and I dab again. He looks tired. I open my laptop and begin to type:

I didn't hear you come in last night?

He bends across me to look at the screen. He smells of sweat and the cowshed, and her.

'I stayed at Clodagh's last night,' he says.

That's three nights this week, I type.

He gives me a look.

Is it serious? I search his face as he stoops once more to read the screen. I want to stroke his dark curls, bury my nose in the nape of his neck like I used to when he was a baby and smell his sweetness.

Now it's Matthew who stares out of the window across the jigsaw of green where the cows are beginning to graze after two hours' milking.

'We get along well, that's all,' he says.

She's a lot older than you, I type.

'Does that matter? Dad was ten years older than you; it's just the same in reverse, that's all. I like her,' he says. 'She feels familiar.'

I say no more after that. The cat jumps back on the bed and starts to settle herself next to me. The day has begun and she's ready for sleep. I wait for Matthew to leave the room before easing myself out of bed. It's serious, I think, and dress in nondescript clothes – a brown woollen skirt and navy roll-neck sweater. It's been a long time since I've been moved to take action. I have a sudden urge to clear cupboards and redecorate, purge clutter from the past. Spring fever. Adrenaline. I decide to invite the girl for supper.

An hour later, I drive away from the farm towards Penzance to buy provisions. It is a beautiful day and the verges wave armfuls of cow parsley, bluebells and pink campion. The moors, which appeared onion-skin brown a month ago, are now a carpet of pink and yellow thrift, heather and gorse. You loved this time of year when flowers push their anthers to the wind. A brazen act, you would say, like the two of us.

I'm heading for the big stores on the outskirts of town. I prefer them to the small shops, enjoying the anonymity and lack of human contact. The doctors said I was lucky. The stroke paralysed my vocal chords and one side of my face only. The face you loved to watch because it reminded you of wind on the water. You said you could see a squall approaching by the seech and gurnall of emotion riffling across my countenance, darkening my eyes and eddying around my mouth. The mouth you kissed with the incredulity of a man bewitched; a mouth now ugly in repose and grotesque in action. When I smile, it strains in one direction like torn rubber caught in a barbed wire fence. I have turned all mirrors to the wall, but still I see the horror of what I have become reflected in the furtive eyes of strangers. In the supermarket, I can at least scuttle through in an unremarkable fashion, lizard-like, darting from aisle to aisle, blending in with the tea, coffee and frozen vegetables. I am still coming to terms with this newfound reticence, this desire to be nobody.

I was lucky, they say. They do not know me.

I drive through New Mill, past the sign to Ding Dong that used to make me smile, and begin to plan a menu in my head: salmon mousse to start, followed by spiced Moroccan lamb and a lemon posset for pudding, to clear the palate. My first stop will be Cornwall Farmers to buy poison for the bait boxes. The rats have been bad on the farm this year; it's the chicken food that attracts them. I will buy paint at B&Q, before stopping off at the big new Sainsbury's on the old Isles of Scilly helicopter site. I might buy Matthew some new clothes. He will like that.

CLODAGH

FOG STOLE off the sea and swallowed the landscape, filling the high-banked lanes like milk. Clodagh searched for a landmark: a farm gate, a wind-sculpted tree, a lichen-clad mound of granite – some talisman from the past upon which to anchor her sight – but the once familiar road had disappeared. It could do that, sea fog. Creep in. It would have started as a thin white line, way out past Longships, and a heralding chill as the fog bank swelled across Mount's Bay heading for land. The sheer speed at which a warm day in West Penwith could be erased never failed to surprise her.

The taxi driver wiped the inside of the car windscreen with a purple bar towel and lowered his window to dab at the side mirror. A blast of Atlantic air filled the cab. She closed her eyes against the seaweed breeze. Tiredness lapped. Memories jostled, tangled as the strandline after a high tide; swimming at Sennen, sand-blasted picnics, fishing in rock pools.

'Your first time in Cornwall?'

She opened her eyes. The driver was watching her in his rear-view mirror.

'Yes,' she lied.

'Down on holiday?'

She nodded.

'Shame to arrive on a night like this, though. It'll look different in the morning, you'll see. Staying at the Tinner's then, are you?'

Ahead, something tall and white reared out of the mist. The timber signpost to Gurnard's Head and Zennor pointing the way with weathered boards and faded script. The fog thinned and the landscape made brief appearances as the car began its slow descent off Penwith Moor towards the coast. A fragment of pasture, a wind-bent hawthorn, a standing stone. The tower of Zennor Church. Her father's hand in hers as they stood to sing his favourite hymn. She hummed, quietly, beneath the whine of the engine.

> Eternal Father, strong to save
> Whose arm hath bound the restless wave
> Who bidd'st the mighty ocean deep
> Its own appointed limits keep.

Five minutes later, she stood alone outside the Tinner's Arms. The pub sign creaked as it swung from a gallows post above her, and she could hear the low murmur of voices inside. Across the road a flight of steps, rounded by the footfall of centuries, rose towards the dark tower of St Senara's Church, which peered down at the pub through the mist. In the morning, if the light were right, she would photograph the graveyard. She loved the unkempt wildness of the place; a circular Bronze Age field strewn with storm-green granite headstones tilted like the wonky teeth of giants. To the north-east, the rolling moors of West Penwith climbed skywards above the tombstones in russet mounds of bracken and furze. Sometimes at dawn or dusk the moors appeared flame red against the blue. To the south-west, a granite-edged patchwork of fields spread out across the coastal lowlands and fell into the sea beyond Zennor.

Clodagh picked up her bags and started to walk away from the pub, past the church, towards the rhythmic pounding of the ocean.

> O hear us when we cry to thee
> For those in peril on the sea.

MATTHEW

MATTHEW TREWHELLA hugged himself in the cold March air. It was six a.m. and the cows were taking their time, their Friesian frames swaying large out of the gloom.

'No hurry, girls!'

He glanced up at a red-tinged mackerel sky. There would be rain later. His father had been a fisherman and taught him how to read the clouds, although Matt had not inherited his father's call to the sea. Instead, at the age of three, he discovered tractors when his Uncle Pat swung him way up high into the rattling cab of a blue Massey Ferguson. It had smelled of mud and diesel, and driving along with his hands on the juddering wheel, and Pat's arms wrapped around him, he had felt like a king. Still did.

Something caught Matt's eye. The cows had seen it too and paused to stare, mid-amble. A woman's torso appeared to glide along the top of a hedge, humming a tune. A minute later, her legs and body became united in the gateway, where she paused to look at him.

'Morning!' he called, raising an arm in her direction. He didn't know her, but thought it polite to acknowledge another person that early in the day.

'Morning,' she said with a brief smile, before melting away down the lane towards the coastal path. She wore an old waxed coat and walking boots, and her hair was as wild, dark and tangled as a clump of bladderwrack. He should have said something, made a joke about being up early, engaged her in conversation. Damn it. He stamped his feet and rubbed his hands. Too late now.

The milking shed was warm with forty head of cattle munching and breathing. Steam rose from the cows' flanks and small misty clouds puffed intermittently from moist, dark nostrils. Matt never tired of the scents and sounds, the smell of sanitation, cows' breath and sweet haylage. The hum of the milking machine as it wheezed and pumped rhythmically like the embryo of a song. It was only as he wiped the cows' udders clean and attached clusters of milking cups with an attendant suck and hiss that he remembered the name of the tune the woman had been humming. It was the fishermen's hymn, his father's favourite. The one they sang at his funeral. Before long he was singing 'Eternal Father' to the cows, and they turned their soft bovine eyes towards him and pricked their ears.

CLODAGH

ST SENARA'S was quiet, as though the church had sunk to the bottom of a shallow sea allowing rays of light, not sound, to drift through its jewelled windows. Clodagh sat in her special chair, the one guarded by a mermaid rising through the dark-grained surface of the wooden bench-end and fish swimming along the embroidered seat cushion. Her father used to call her his little mermaid on the days he was on dry land. Sundays, mostly. The day fishermen went to church, mended nets and sang shanties in-the-round at the pub after tea. Some days, her mother would take her to listen, when the weather was warm and the men sang outside on the quay at Newlyn. Her dad led the singing in a strong clear voice, and the others replied. Call and reply. Call and reply. Like the rhythm of waves arriving and retreating across a beach. When he sang 'Trelawney' the men would puff up with Cornish pride; when he sang 'The White Rose' all the women cried.

In winter, they'd stay in by the fires her mother built with intricate care, using bone-dry kindling laid in neat parallel piles, like her ironing.

'The trouble with your mother is she has a folding disease,' her father had announced one day. They had laughed, the three of them, really laughed. But her mother should have known. That tiny observance, an annoyance dressed up as a joke. It had been a sign.

The church darkened as a cloud moved in front of the sun and she saw her mother's face, the colour of a pale listless sea at dawn, the day her father left.

That afternoon, Clodagh retraced her steps along the coast path, detouring to Pendour Cove to photograph treasure from the strandline. She found a prickly shore urchin feasting on a crop of barnacles, and a smooth white cuttlebone – her father had called them 'swans' breasts' – which she pocketed. The sand was littered with tiger-striped limpet shells and the abandoned porcelain houses of cockles and dog whelks. She arranged her trove in a shallow rock pool decorated with red dulse and pale green sea lettuce. The rain had stopped and light broke through a violet sky, illuminating the water and its contents. Setting the Pentax 50mm lens to rapid-fire, she captured the liquid bowl of treasure for eternity. Then, with a sharp knife, she scraped a crop of tide-washed mussels off the rocks into a carrier bag for her tea before climbing back up the steep cliff path towards Treen.

It was five o'clock by the time she reached the farm and Matt was closing the yard gates after the second milking session of the day. She saw him gathering his mouth in readiness to speak, but she smiled and strolled on past the farm before he had a chance to utter a word.

Clodagh repeated her daily walks to Treen and back. On the third day there was a loud shout above the rattle of a diesel engine.

'Hey, you!'

She turned and saw Matt leaning out of the cab of a green and yellow John Deere tractor. He cut the engine.

'Are you from around here?'

'Not really,' she said. 'I'm renting a cottage at Zennor for a few months … taking a bit of a sabbatical.'

'Oh yes? What do you do?'

'I'm a photographer.'

'Really? Sounds interesting,' said Matt.

Clodagh waited for him to ask the inevitable.

'Are you down here on your own?'

'I am,' she said, suppressing a smile. At least he hadn't asked her if she was single.

'Can I … would you mind if I asked you out for a drink? Just as a friend, you know … sorry, that sounds really crass.'

'That would be nice,' she said. 'Shall I meet you at the Tinner's Arms at, say, seven o'clock tonight?'

MATTHEW

MATT ARRIVED early at the Tinner's Arms and made his way to the bar, nodding his head to a few locals as he went – old Major Berryman with his Daily Telegraph, whisky and black Labrador at his feet, and the Davey brothers from Boswednack Farm, with a couple of girls from the vets.

'Pint of Tribute please, Jonno,' he said. He leaned sideways into the bar, whilst keeping an eye on the door.

Jonno was an old school friend and had played prop forward for the Pirates prior to a busted knee. The conversation began with rugby, before moving to football, cows and the weather. Matt tried not to glance at his watch until, two pints later, the door creaked open and a vision in sea-green silk walked in.

He waved her over.

'Hello,' he said, as he kissed her on both cheeks, whilst thanking the Lord for Dutch courage. 'I'm Matt, by the way.'

'Clodagh,' she replied. 'And it's a whisky and Canada Dry for me, please,' she said, addressing Jonno.

'I think you're the tallest woman I've ever kissed,' said Matt – he was cruising now – 'and the most beautiful.'

'I'll second that,' said Jonno from the bar, as he poured ginger ale from a dizzy height onto a shot of whisky. 'Ice, my beauty?'

Clodagh led the way, glass in hand, to a crackling fire at the back of the pub. She settled herself down on a worn leather sofa where Matt joined her. He tried not to stare down her cleavage and fixed his eyes on her legs, which she crossed towards him, hitching up her dress to reveal a shapely pair of knees and bare skin. He averted his gaze and stared into the fire. A grandfather clock struck eight from the corner of the room.

She leaned over and pressed her hand on his arm.

'It was kind of you to invite me out tonight,' she said. 'I was ready for some company. Shells and seaweed are great to photograph, but they don't talk much. So, tell me about yourself.'

Matt took a long sip of beer and began to relax. He told her about the farm and his cows and his mother and uncle. They ordered more drinks and scampi and chips, and he talked about his love of the church and the choir, which he sang in most Sundays. And how he wanted to walk the Cornish coastline from Bude on the north coast to Saltash on the south.

'I never go for walks,' he said. 'Stupid, isn't it, living here? But that's farmers for you. Plus, the collies don't do walks; they herd sheep.'

He watched her face melt into ripples as she laughed. This moment is perfect, he thought. Just perfect.

'You haven't mentioned your father,' she said.

'He died. A couple of years ago now. Heart attack. He was a lot older than Mum, mind. Always had a weak heart.'

'I'm sorry,' said Clodagh.

'No. It was probably the best way to go – I mean, if there's such a thing as a good way, then that would be it, wouldn't it? They say drowning is peaceful, but I don't know. I'd rather go out with a bang, myself.'

They both fell silent and watched the red dance of embers until

Matt cleared his throat to speak again.

'Dad loved the sea. He lived on that boat of his. Made me feel bad, really, because he would have liked me to be a fisherman. Not that he made me feel bad, he wasn't the type, but, well, you know, it's always when they're gone you wish you'd spent more time with them.'

She was watching him and he returned her gaze. It was only then he noticed her eyes were the colour of pale green sea glass.

They met at the Tinner's Arms every night for a week. The night Clodagh told him she was an orphan, he kissed her on the lips. To his amazement, she kissed him back. They bypassed the pub and strolled, hand-in-hand, beyond the church along a rutted track to a small granite cottage hunkered down at the edge of the village. Matt kissed her again on the age-worn doorstep and once more in the hallway, which smelled of old coats and damp carpet. She took his hand and led him upstairs to her low-ceilinged bedroom where the air smelled of just-washed laundry.

'Mind your head,' she said, as she shrugged her dress to the floor and stepped naked from a pool of silk, before drawing him to her on the bed.

'What happened to your parents?'

'Sshhh. No more talking.'

Matt searched her eyes. Strains of the fishermen's hymn echoed in his head as she trailed her hair across his skin. Trailed and stroked, trailed and stroked. Conjuring a storm within his gentle soul.

CLODAGH

IT WAS mid-afternoon and a pale meringue of sun hung low in a grey-whipped sky. Clodagh sat cross-legged amongst the tomb-stones of St Senara's churchyard staring up at the moors. She was thinking about Matthew Trewhella. She had imagined him the age she first found him, a newborn resting between the lines of the

Zennor Parish Births and Deaths Register. In reality, he was all grown up and big as a bull. Gentle, too. She hadn't expected that. He had inherited her father's height and his mother's good looks.

She inclined her head towards a pale blue ginger jar sitting on the grass beside her and removed the lid to survey the contents.

'Happy now, Mum? The Siren of Treen can't smile or speak. She's as shrivelled and dried up as a mermaid's purse on the strandline.'

A lone curlew wheeled and cried above the moor. Clodagh rocked back and forth to keep warm. Rocked and hummed. Rocked and hummed. Some sounds were lonely … she reached her hand into the ginger jar … the braying of a donkey, the mewl of a buzzard, the moan of a foghorn off Land's End. She stirred her fingers through the ash and thought about the night before. Matt's hands. They had been wide as spades, and warm and dry across her skin. Comforting. His hands had felt like home.

She shivered. She had been sitting on the ground too long and her legs were numb.

'I should have done this twenty years ago,' she said, picking up the ginger jar and removing the lid. Then she sang the last verse of the only hymn she knew and scattered her mother's dusty remains amongst the tombstones of Zennor.

MORWENNA

'SMELLS GOOD, Ma,' Matthew says later that afternoon as he pops his head around the back door. I know by the way he's bending his tall body through the door-frame his boots are caked in mud, and he still has chores to do in the yard. I ask him what time she's coming and he says six, and that he'll be done in a second and in to take a shower.

They say spriggans steal babies from prams, and replace them with one of their own changelings. Do you remember how I used to place sprays of rowan in Matthew's pram and turn his little cardigans inside out to protect him? He's been safe all these years, our beautiful boy. I add more lemon juice to the salmon mousse and dip my finger in to taste. I can still taste, but eating is slow. She's no spriggan, this girl; they're ugly little things, spriggans. No, you bred a Siren, my love. A big, beautiful Siren and she's come back for him. I fold in a little gelatine and beat the pink mixture to a pulp, before distributing it into ramekin dishes, which I place in the fridge.

There's a chill in the dining room, even in May. The granite floors draw winter in at any time of year, despite a scattering of rugs. Only the kitchen stays warm with the range. I left the interconnecting door to the dining room open all afternoon to air the place, and I have lit a fire. The table is laid and there are flowers – bluebells and hyacinths. There's a photograph of you on the mantelpiece, taken on our honeymoon. She will go straight to it, of course. She might even pick it up. I'm ready for that. Prepared for her hands to caress your face. I know what she'll be thinking and that she will say nothing, and neither will I.

An hour later, Matthew has gone to fetch the girl. There are welcoming candles lit in the porch and on the windowsills. The Moroccan lamb casserole is resting in the warming oven. I have nothing more to do but crush the final ingredients with a pestle and mortar: lemon zest, garlic and herbs, to be added as a garnish.

I have taken care with my appearance, tonight. Remember that purple velvet dress the colour of nightshade? It still fits, still shows off my legs and my décolletage, where men dropped their eyes and you dropped your kisses. Deadly, you called me, as you peeled the velvet from my skin. My hair has faded to a rope of grey, a moonshine pelt, loosened and falling in waves down my back. My eyes, lost almost to the grief of losing you, are still there amongst the creases. Still casting their indigo gaze across the room to your face in the tarnished silver frame on the mantelpiece. My lips? An angry gash of Dior red.

Candles gutter as a door opens in another part of the house.

'Are you warding off spirits?' a voice booms from the hallway.

My brother, Pat, walks into the kitchen, his just-shaved face gleaming, his cheeks ruddy with warmth and sixty years on the bottle. He gives me a peck on both cheeks. He smells of aftershave and I recoil. I invited him to fill gaps in conversation, not to flirt with the guests.

'Never seen so many candles lit, gal,' he says with a chuckle. 'Am I here for supper or a séance?'

I pour Pat a whisky. We don't like each other much, but he lets me live in the house, and I'm grateful for that. Said he preferred the village. Bought himself a little cottage down the road in Treen with some money Pa left us. Gives him a break from the cows, he says, but I know it's the pub on the doorstep that clinched the deal.

I hear the thud of a car door closing and the dogs barking. Matthew's here with the girl. I go to the front door to greet them. She's even taller than I expected, wearing a charcoal trouser suit with an elegant, tailored jacket and cream satin blouse, her dark gypsy hair piled high. She means business, this girl. Clodagh. There's no denying she's beautiful. She's brought a bottle of champagne and a bouquet of white lilies. Matthew introduces us on the doorstep and I nod my head in silent greeting. Clodagh hesitates, and I usher them into the hallway, giving her no chance to shake my hand or present the flowers.

'It's good to meet you, Mrs Trewhella,' she says in the hallway. We look at each other. I proffer my ugliness like a grizzly prize and stare her down. Behind the artifice of a beautiful smile, her past rears up to greet me. Images flash: your hand in hers, the church at Zennor, a child swinging her feet in the mermaid's chair, her mother's pain, the orphanage and foster homes, the bitterness of years held back. The madness. Controlled. Everything is planned and under control with this one. She must know that a gift of lilies for the hostess heralds bad luck.

There is an acrid smell in the air. I have forgotten the toast under the grill and hurry into the kitchen, avoiding the girl's second attempt to hand me the flowers. Charcoal peppers the ceramic sink as I chip at the burnt toast. Matthew carries the flowers and champagne into the kitchen and holds up the bottle with a questioning look. I shake my head and point towards the fridge. This is not the time for celebration – not yet, and I have white wine chilled and ready to serve with the first course.

The salmon mousse is laid out on the table, and I show Clodagh to her seat whilst Matthew pours the wine. I take a long sip of Sauvignon Blanc and watch her. She has the cool, measured air of someone who has suffered and survived.

'You have a beautiful home, Mrs Trewhella,' she says. She scrapes a translucent line of salmon across half a triangle of toast. She eats like a bird.

'I'm sure Mum wouldn't mind if you call her Morwenna,' says Matthew. 'You don't mind, do you, Ma?'

He looks at me across the table. I shake my head. One night of informality won't hurt.

When the first course is finished I insist upon clearing the plates myself. I serve up the Moroccan lamb with couscous, setting Clodagh's plate to one side. Sour cream makes a good accompaniment to spice. I mix a teaspoon of finely chopped garlic to a dollop of sour cream and swirl the mixture through Clodagh's food. I add plain sour cream to the other three plates, and a sprinkle of lemon zest to all four portions, before carrying them to the table. Clodagh thanks me, but says it's too much and passes the plate to Matthew, whereupon I whip it away from him and return from the kitchen with a slightly smaller portion for her. The men don't seem to notice. Pat is reminiscing about his rugby days, and Matthew is teasing him. Clodagh is laughing, but I know she has sensed my irritation. With a voice and a smile, I could have made light of my actions. I could have said, 'That's all right, dear, but Matthew will want twice that amount.' Without speech, my actions seem crude and remonstrative. I ladle an overly large amount of lamb onto Matthew's plate to make a point.

'What's this, Ma?' he says. 'Are you trying to make me grow taller?'

The cat skulks past the open dining room door and pauses to freeze us with an emerald stare. Then she turns and leaves. She is heading for the cat flap with six hours of murder in mind.

Plates are scraped clean and the men mumble their approval. Clodagh helps me clear. We are alone at last in the kitchen. I could open my laptop and blow her cover. I could write in black marker pen across the fridge door, I KNOW WHO YOU ARE. Instead, I open the fridge and remove four lemon possets. I hand each one to Clodagh who places them on the gold-edged Wedgwood saucers I have laid out on the kitchen table. I hand her a packet of brandy-snap biscuits and she knows to place a couple on the side of each saucer. We could be mother and daughter, I think. And I feel nothing.

Clodagh offers to carry the desserts through to the dining room, but I shake my head, indicating that I will follow her through with a tray. I watch her go – a black shadow in stilettos crossing the hallway. For a moment, I sense the wildness of their love and the spell she casts over my son when her hair comes down and the stilettos are peeled off slowly, from heel to elegant toe. I imagine her pale satin blouse sliding over her breasts like poured cream, and his tongue upon them. And, worse still, I imagine him gone from me and inside her.

I pick up one lemon posset and replace it with a different one from the back of the fridge. Then I take some tiny bells of pink heather from a sprig I have in a jam jar at the kitchen window and decorate three of the desserts for luck and safekeeping. I adorn the fourth lemon posset with a cluster of blue rosemary flowers. I have always grown rosemary beside the front door – they say it wards off witches and bad spirits. I picked a bunch this afternoon, burying my nose into the dark, spiky foliage to inhale the pungent smell of spring before chopping up a handful to add to the Moroccan lamb. I saved some flowers for now, floated in an eggcup of water to keep them fresh.

I carry the tray of desserts through to the dining room. Pat is telling Clodagh a story we have heard a hundred times, when the brakes failed on his tractor and he almost ended up in the sea. He was saved by a metal blade of the plough, which caught on a lump of Penwith granite at the edge of the cliff and stopped the tractor dead. Pat's drunk, and he slurs his way through the finale, roaring with laughter at the tale of his near demise. I can tell by the angle and slight movement of Matthew's arm that he is stroking Clodagh beneath the table. Walking to the end of the room, I place the tray on the sideboard and go to stoke the fire. There's no hurry, I think, taking care not to look at your face on the mantelpiece. I hand out the lemon desserts: heather to safe-keep the boys and rosemary to ward off the girl.

If I could smile, I would.

BALLAST

SARAH THOMAS

THEY HALTED by Fox's Shipping Office, its long bay windows affording a clear view of the harbour and its business. Beyond the moored sloops and fishing boats, Maria Maddern could see two steamships at anchor in the bay. Her gardener Pascoe slid gratefully out of the saddle and took the horses. A gig cut a direct line across the water towards them, ferrying men and goods to shore. A long, fully-loaded barge made its way slowly upriver to Penryn. Gulls screamed, mobbing a fish catch.

A slight, tanned man, compact in blue serge, immediately picked his way through the groups gathered on the building's wide flight of steps and approached the riders. Maria dismounted and raised a hand in acknowledgement.

'Captain Smythe – glad to see you, sir.'

The captain looked keenly into her face, taking her gloved hand in his. 'Miss Maddern, good day to you.'

'Good passage, I hope?'

He smiled. 'Matthews, fetch Miss Maddern her packets.'

'Aye, Cap'n.' A sailor in attendance turned smartly back inside.

'No Master Frederick with you today?'

'This morning he pruned one of my mother's larch trees with an ill-aimed shot and I chose not to have his company.' Her voice didn't quite achieve the lightness of tone she had intended. 'Perhaps you could offer my brother a position as crew on your next voyage – though I cannot vouch for his usefulness.'

The sailor had returned. He coughed quietly, offering some oiled cloth parcels. Smythe presented them to her with a small bow. Maria smoothed her hands over the sea-stained label of the uppermost package. New seed varieties from the Far East, an unnamed species promising to rank her garden with that of Mr Fox at Penjerrick, or those at Glendurgan and Trebah. Smythe leaned forward. 'There are some unseen beauties in there, according to my man.' The captain's voice softened. 'No doubt your Mr Pascoe will work his magic.' He turned to acknowledge the waiting gardener.

But Pascoe had left the horses and his angular frame was poised on the edge of the granite quay like a heron. As they watched, he attempted to snatch something low in the water with one hand, while securing himself with a sinewy arm around a mooring rope. 'Careful, man!' Smythe started forward. The old man almost lost his grip and had to strain hard to heave himself back to safety. Was he feeling his age at last? she wondered.

'What are you after there, Mr Pascoe?'

Pascoe pointed silently as he regained both breath and dignity. There were dark logs floating amongst the moored boats, nudging against the quayside, bobbing, crowding this corner of the harbour. Brown stumps, soft and barkless.

'Do you know what they are, Captain?' She stared as hard as the older man.

'Why, that's ballast, Miss, tossed overboard. Off the Lady Jocelyn.' Smythe nodded in the direction of the steamship anchored out in the bay alongside his own ship. 'Arrived from New South Wales just yesterday. They'll not need the extra weight once she picks up her next load of passengers at Plymouth.'

Pascoe pushed himself back up on his knees. 'Can we fish one out, sir?'

Smythe whistled and gestured. A boy emerged from the chaos of nearby nets and pots, and after brief exchange of coin, launched himself shuddering into the dark water and hooked a floating log towards him. It rolled under his hands, dense with fine roots.

'You'll be needing a net, sir. 'Tis too 'eavy.'

Pascoe tossed a short length of netting down and the trunk was snared and hauled to their feet. Maria crouched to study it. At its pointed crown, small bright green tendrils were growing, seeking light.

'Why, it's some kind of fern, isn't it, Mr Pascoe?' She ran her fingers over its unfamiliar texture; its wiry roundness made her think of a hibernating animal. An unfamiliar species of the antipodean world was suddenly right there in her hands. She was aware of her gardener's intense scrutiny and smiled.

Smythe was immediately brisk with enthusiasm and the possibility of a little shore business. 'Let us call on the Jocelyn's captain. He'll tell us what these are. Wells, send word ahead to Cap'n Nash we're on our way.'

Maria took Captain Smythe's arm and they walked the short distance to the Fox Offices. Pipe smoke hung heavy above the heads of agents, captains and merchants. The talk was of prices, weather, timings. A rumble of male voices. A nod of heads as they entered.

'Cap'n Nash, may I introduce Miss Maddern? She has taken an interest in your waste ballast.'

Nash stepped forward. Another tanned, weathered face and a pair of observant eyes.

'Ah, let me wager you're considering the possibility of growing they tree ferns.' The voice was amused, Nash not unused to the enthusiasms of his county's gentry for growing exotics of all kinds. He nodded in the direction of the quay where the logs were just visible alongside the waterline of a barge, a sleek dark pod of movement.

'Do you think they'll take here in Cornwall?' Her eyes were drawn back to Pascoe, who was directing the boy to fish yet another specimen out of the water.

'I do not see why not. Good shelter, plenty of rain. In Australia they grow oh … so high.' He gestured airily towards the ornate plaster ceiling and she visualised a green umbrella of fronds arching above her head. As they both watched Pascoe's progress with a second catch, she estimated the possible volume of the floating logs.

'Has anyone else tried yet?'

'Not that I've heard. Certainly not in Cornwall.'

'So I'll need a barge.'

'Miss?' Nash strained to catch her purpose.

'I want all of them, Captain. I can picture a forest of tree ferns at the bottom of my valley. I want to create our very own New South Wales in the Helford.'

Nash raised an eyebrow. 'Every one of them?' But Smythe was quick to make an offer of support. 'Let me help you with transport, Miss Maddern. I'll arrange for the ferns to be loaded and see them across the bay tomorrow.'

'Thank you. Well, we must be going.' The two men watched her walk quickly away, clutching her packets of seeds, to her waiting man and horses.

Light rain darkened the necks of the horses as they began the long ride back to the Helford. At last the granite gateposts of the estate came into sight and they paused, as was their habit, to look down into the garden. Pascoe shifted in the saddle, easing his stiffness. Maria gazed at the maze of lush exotics and lost paths with exasperation, felt the weight of it pushing, leaning on her as if she were at the tiller of a boat working against a strong current. She reflected on her hasty decision to buy the ballast. Would the ferns transform the landscape in the way she desired? She was determined to have her own triumphs, she knew that much. She nudged the tired mare forward with a touch of the heels.

The morning was lively. The captain had accompanied the barge to oversee delivery of its cargo to the Maddern estate, which, like its neighbours, used the sheltered coves of the Helford estuary to receive goods by sea. Falmouth watermen eased the boat into the shallows, allowing Smythe to wade ashore.

Maria stood waiting on the grey shingle, wrapped in a wool shawl against the wind. She watched his wet boots leave a quick, dark trail across the stones. 'Good as your word, Captain.' She couldn't help but like his ebullience, despite the fact that he had made profit from her impatience for new plants once again.

The water soon bobbed with logs, tossed overboard from the barge. Two boys lunged about in the shallows like dolphins driving a shoal. Pascoe hunkered at the top of the slipway, long legs folded beneath him. He held a bucket ready to sluice the stacked ferns with fresh stream water.

John Maddern, mine owner, widower, a man who prided himself on being of a measured temperament, had walked down through the garden to observe proceedings. Maria could see her father's irritation in his walk, hands thrust into coat pockets, massaging a gut twisted with indigestion and disappointment. She knew he felt his expectations of his daughter to be reasonable – marriage, a connected family seat, children. She, however, mourned his abandonment of the garden that her parents had begun together.

The discussion over dinner last night had quickly slipped into a terse fusillade of facts and consequences. Fred had related the incident with the larch tree and the gun and she knew her father's equilibrium would be tested today by this, the cost of a barge from Falmouth full of waste ballast. Her impulse was to retreat into the cool green clearings.

'So you and my daughter have hatched yet another scheme, Smythe?' His tone was jovial, but Maria could see that the hand-shake was over-firm in its unspoken annoyance. 'More plants, I see? Maria has taken root here in this damned garden.'

'Captain Nash assures me no one has tried growing tree ferns yet. I think she's onto something quite special here, sir.' Maria was familiar with the way Smythe nurtured competition between landowners to ensure a market for his trade, but noted his quick support with surprise. He had, after all, secured his business.

'A tour, perhaps, Captain?'

The three of them made a way through a forest of bamboos, arching stems rustling in the breeze, dried pale leaves creating a soft littered floor under their boots. The September sun glinted on waxy camellia leaves. Chinese maples blushed crimson with the change of the season. Seed pods were swelling on the branches of maturing magnolias. Water trickled downhill in tiny runnels, joining a small stream they had to bridge with long steps. The garden scented and greened the air around them.

Smythe nodded appreciatively as they navigated the more accessible paths contouring the valley slopes, shouldering past unchecked foliage. Catching the scent of barber's soap as she stepped behind him, Maria tried to visualise the captain's hard journeying to Canton and Shanghai. She had read newspaper accounts of crews decimated by malaria, ships lost to piracy, and yet he had made many successful passages in recent years.

'Do you think there'll be a time when passengers like myself could visit the Far East and look for ourselves at its natural wonders, Captain?'

'Dear God, Maria, is there no end to this obsession?' Her father halted abruptly on the path. Smythe diplomatically offered no encouragement for this particular plan. They arrived back at the beach.

'I have no doubt your Australian exotics will succeed, Miss Maddern. I look forward to visiting when the Esperanza is next in harbour.'

Maria watched the powerful heave of shoulders in unison as sailors raised the sails and the barge moved slowly offshore, bound for Falmouth. Smythe stood braced in the stern, smartly saluting her ambitions.

'You do know,' he suddenly cupped his hands to carry his voice across the widening water, 'there are berths open on SS Jocelyn. She'll be sailing from Plymouth in two weeks.'

She was held by the amused challenge in his eyes and registered her father's sharp intake of breath.

Maria thought of the coming autumn in the garden. The tree ferns bedded in, drinking the soft rain from the west, sheltered in the shade of the pines above, forming a jungle canopy. Her father went indoors and she was alone. She walked briskly, feeling lighter in mood than she had for weeks, excited by the potential of these new plants. Smythe's comment drifted around in the back of her mind.

She followed the path around the pond to the fern stack, and there she saw Pascoe, leaning back against the plants. A single log had been upended and planted in a shallow bed, its growing tip pointing to the sunlight – ballast metamorphosing into plant. She looked from fern to gardener and saw that here too was change. Life had slipped quietly away.

'Mr Pascoe?' Maria came closer than she'd ever been in her life to that familiar face. She reached out and touched his shoulder, already knowing that she wouldn't wake him now. She studied his calloused hands, work-thickened fingers and nails rimmed with soil. She was reminded of the great sycamore they had lost last winter, felled by high winds, heartwood rotting within.

He had taught her to look for the signs of a diseased plant, the tinge and shift of colour, the curl and wilt of fresh leaves. She had not observed him carefully enough, she knew. He'd never see the ferns grow, nor glory in their giant stature. Her loss welled larger, sharper, as she thought of her own future.

The low afternoon sunlight dropped shadows.

Behind her the garden settled, but down at the beach waves murmured insistently, and the tide was turning.

I RUN IN GRAVEYARDS

CLARE HOWDLE

I RUN in graveyards. I am the sort of person who runs in grave-yards. What does that say about me? I know what the lady with the dachshund thinks it says. And the woman with the pram. But why is running any worse than walking a dog? Or pushing a screaming baby? It's vital. Running is vital. I can't think of anywhere more appropriate to run. Really.

I am thirty-four years old and four people in my life have died. Well five, I suppose. Four people close to me. And this. The reason I'm not running right now. The reason I'm sitting here. With all this time to think.

GRANDAD

I'M GOING to start with Grandad. Because almost everyone has one. Grandads are old. Sometimes very old. Like mine. We knew he was going to die. It wasn't quite when we thought, but we knew. A week away from his ninetieth birthday. He tried, but he couldn't hold on any longer. You always know with a grandad. Because they are old. Sometimes very old.

That didn't stop it from being sad. I hated seeing him like that. In the hospital. He was so small. Drowning in his sheets as he used the bed button to fold himself in half, up and down, up and down, to try and make me smile.

It felt real, the sadness, while I was there. We were standing right by him. I had my hand on his, fingertips touching the drip. But he was so far away. It felt more real still as I walked out of the ward. And it swelled in my throat as I drove home on my own. In the rain.

I sat on the sofa with gin in a mug and told Alex how Grandad was going to die. And I cried. But I was crying because of the gin. And because I felt guilty that I'm not the sort of person who calls their grandad every week. Or month even. And that the last time I spoke to him was in between work calls because Dad said he was going in for his operation and it would be good if I called. So I did. But even while I was talking I was thinking about something else.

He talked about jam. Around the back of Grandad's sheltered housing estate was a massive blackberry bush, grown so thick it was eating up the pavement that skirted the feeder road for the A39. The berries were probably toxic. He would pick those blackberries every year and make his 'secret recipe' jam. The council had got hedge trimmers in to cut it down. On the call, Grandad was apologising to me. He'd tried to stop them – whatever that means – but there was nothing he could do. 'No jam this year,' he said. Which was absurd because he still had shelves full in his tiny bedsit, with its shiny, shiny sink and crease-free duvet. And prize roses out front. He probably slept on jars of blackberry jam.

So we talked about jam and about cat-hair radios, I think, or something like that. And I acted normal. And he acted normal. It was all normal. And then he died. One week after.

At his funeral everyone smiled when they saw us, the family, I mean. But their lips were glued together and their eyes were wet. The Masons sang a song when the readings finished. It seemed impromptu. Dad held it together, Irene said. He did seem together. I've no idea how I seemed. The view from the crematorium was beautiful – out over the plot, across Glynn Valley, green fields, stretching trees, blue sky.

When we all left, the girls – us girls – we said goodbye to Grandad. To the coffin. I don't know who started it, but we sort of filed up, in procession. Laura's neck was red. I held her hand. Then I touched the coffin. I held my free hand on the varnished wood and felt how cold it was under my fingers. After the touch, I backed away, letting my fingers linger. It felt like something someone in a film would do.

I am the sort of person who runs in graveyards.

THOMAS

WHEN I was little – like eleven – a boy I knew got cancer. He was the first person I ever knew to get it. At least I think it was cancer. But I might be remembering it wrong. We were friends, actually. He wasn't just a boy I knew. We were friends. He saved a seat for me when we had to go to the TV room after break time to watch How We Used to Live. I sat down next to him and crossed my legs then pretended to concentrate on the TV and not on Debbie, or Joanne or Anna, who I usually sat with, as I was sure they would be laughing at me. He held my hand once. In the Victorian episode where the family get sent to the poorhouse. I think he thought I was sad. His fingers were cold and his eyes were big and so, so brown and he asked me if I was okay and I shrugged and tried to look sadder, because even though he wasn't Chris Collier I didn't want him to stop holding my hand.

He invited me to his house for tea after that. Not the same day or anything but soon after, a week maybe. It was afternoon break and we were playing Bulldog and I was leaning against the wire fence at the end of the playground, panting, with my hands on my knees. He had just run too, but looked fine. He played a lot of football – and was really, really good at it – so Bulldog was easy for him. His face was still pink though, as he leaned on the fence next to me. He kicked the dirt and asked me really quietly, like he didn't want me to hear. I was watching the witchy girl who smelled a bit of wee play hopscotch on her own. 4 5, 6, 7 8, 9 pivot. I waited for her to get all the way back to number 1 before I said yes. I looked him square in the face, with all his freckles and his hair and his big brown eyes and I thought about Debbie and Joanne and Anna and I ignored it all and I said yes. He sort of smiled and said it would be toad-in-the-hole, five o'clock or I could come straight from school, up to me, then ran off into the Bulldog line again.

I didn't go. I didn't tell him I wasn't going to. I just didn't turn up. My mum didn't know to take me because I didn't ask her, although I did think of blaming her, or her car, or my sister or something if he asked me why the next day. When I was eating my tea I thought about him sitting there, next to a laid place, maybe even with toad-in-the-hole on the plate, my toad-in-the-hole, all plump and puffy. It's lucky I didn't go, as I felt sick all night long.

But he didn't ask me. The next day at school. He didn't ask me and he didn't really talk to me any more. Or save me a space in the TV room. He didn't play Bulldog either. And he started coming in less and less.

At secondary school, he was in Geevor and I was in Coates so I didn't see him much. Sometimes in the corridor, sometimes waiting outside the science block. I would smile at him but he would look right through me. He lost his hair, I noticed that. Everyone noticed and everyone talked about it. Then Mrs Harrison came into tutor group – or did she call an assembly? – and told us to sit down and all be quiet and listen because she had sad news. 'Poorly,' she said, which I remember thinking was an odd choice of word, because it made it sound like he had food poisoning or a nasty cold. And they don't make you lose your hair.

Debbie suggested making him a big card and getting everyone in the school to sign it. Her voice was wobbling a bit and Anna was crying.

He died a few weeks later. There was another assembly. Debbie didn't even get to give him the card. They played 'Always Look on the Bright Side of Life' at his funeral. Everyone was crying then, even the teachers. I kept my chin on my chest so my hair hung right over my eyes, but I could still see his coffin as they carried it out. It was really small. I'm not even sure I'm remembering any of this right, or if I'm just making up the details so it feels more meaningful.

I don't even like toad-in-the-hole anyway.

It's not just running in graveyards. Sometimes I spit too. When I'm running I mean. Because my mouth feels full and I can't breathe and so I spit to clear it all out. I bet Debbie and Joanne and Anna have never spat in a graveyard.

ALICE

I WAS twenty-two when my boss died. I was working in London but travelling back almost every weekend. Itching for that first glimpse of the sea at Teignmouth, straining my neck as we crossed the Tamar to see the sign that told me I was home.

She was difficult. No, she was a nightmare. She would tell me that leaving on time meant I wasn't dedicated. That I wasn't cut out for this job. That I should just learn to apply myself. She was twenty-seven. I would watch people subtly shaking their heads in meetings after she spoke or smirking at each other when they heard her on the phone. Everyone thought it. Though no one said it in the church, to her parents, or her fiancé, of course. Once we heard the news, everyone was kind and nice and made her out to be someone she wasn't. People cried then, too. In the office, when they found out. I just sat with my head down, hair covering my eyes. I think I might have smiled when Emma told me. I didn't mean to. It just slipped out. I don't know why. I wasn't happy. I wasn't anything.

She took me into the stairwell between the two floors. It was a strange place to be told something like that. Not really anywhere. I was expecting to be reprimanded for watching Breakfast at Tiffany's on my desk TV again, instead of the network's own channel. But there was no scolding. Instead she just looked at me. Her face was flat and grey and her eyes were like saucers. Talking to me was the first thing she did when she got off the call. She touched my arm. For too long. Her tongue stuck to the roof of her mouth as she spoke. Neither of us knew what we should do.

It was DVT that did it. On the way back from Banff. Alice had broken her leg skiing (which I had been so excited about as it meant she wouldn't be coming into the office for weeks) and they'd told her she couldn't fly. But she demanded to board.

Her fiancé found her on the floor of the bathroom when he came home from work. The clot had worked its way up from her calf to her brain. When the coroner's report came out her face was on the front of all the papers. Because she was only twenty-seven. And her parents were suing the airline.

The ceremony was so long. Catholic. It was raining, I remember that. Someone slipped off the pavement outside the church and had to go to hospital. We all wore black and we all went to the pub after. I left when people starting toasting her.

I had to call all her contacts. And have her email cancelled. And clear out her desk drawers. They smelled of her. There was her brush, still thick with her hair, her perfume, her copy of Summer Brides with pages folded down. Michael came in to collect the box. I couldn't look at him. He said she always talked about me, said I was great to work with. I knew he was lying. I bet he didn't even know my name. People said I was so brave and so capable, because I just kept on doing things, because I didn't let it get to me. But what else do you do in a situation like that? Life goes on.

Life goes on, they say. And I suppose it does. It always did. Apart from last night. Apart from this morning. Sat here, with four other women. All waiting. None of us feel brave right now.

CRAIG

HE WAS the hardest. Because of how it finished with us and how he never really accepted it had and how he was a big part of my life for so long. With Craig I actually cried. I didn't do it to make myself fit in, or hide away so no one could see my face. I put the phone down on his best friend and I ran from the attic office I was in at the time. I ran down to the very end of the pier and let the wind blow the hair into my eyes and my mouth and I swore into the choppy waves and it carried across the estuary, getting lost in the salt and the spray. I cried and I shouted and thrashed at the railings. But not for him, or his mum, or his little brother. I cried because it was absurd. It was pointless and ridiculous and such a waste for anyone to go like that.

He was hit by a lorry on a road in Thailand. A busy road, so busy they left safety flags by the side of it for pedestrians to carry so the traffic would see them as they crossed. But the traffic didn't see Craig. Or his girlfriend. The truck hit them at eighty miles an hour. 'They wouldn't have known what was happening. They wouldn't have felt it.' But we do. We are left to imagine.

So I was crying for that, too. Crying for the scar it would leave on everyone who knew him and the magnitude of a memory like that, which refuses to be let go of. I was swearing into the waves because I thought I had got away. From him, from London, from all of it. I was back home for good. I woke up to the sound of seagulls not sirens. I had a new life. I swam at the beach after work. I ran along the coast path to Swanpool and up, up, up. I didn't want this. To have this. But there it was. A phone call. A lorry. And no way back.

I cried then. I cried on the pier and I cried at home and I cried as I looked through old photographs of us travelling together to send to his mum. And it felt false and selfish, like every tear was a lie running down my cheeks, giving me away. But maybe that's how grief is. Maybe everyone is crying for themselves. Or hiding how they feel. Or wishing they would feel something more.

1/4

I AM crying now. Sitting, with my green folder on my knees. My legs are shaking. They do that when I am anxious. Though I don't know what I'm anxious for. There is no chance of good news here. I know what's happened. So I won't second-guess myself or fake it or think what other people would want me to do or say. I can't feel any more than I do now. I have felt so much in the last twenty-four hours I am still aching from it.

And yes, I am crying for me. And it is selfish. But that is okay. One, two, three, four of us sit there waiting to see the nurse. Waiting for a cold, intrusive scan to pass its verdict. I reach into my pocket for a rag of tissue. Look out the window. The seagulls are circling in the thermals, riding them up, up, up until they are just tiny dots against the infinite sky.

I know I am the one in my four. I hope these other women aren't the one in their fours as well.

Tonight I am going to go for a run.

THE MAPLE IS
IN BLOSSOM

CATHY GALVIN

ON THE ten to ten from Liskeard I remembered the dawn light from your window, jackdaws, a tree breathing in and I told you it was a while since I'd looked at a tree that way. Told you about the blossom on the Canada maple from the window in the house I had sold, all it had breathed on me and my children gone. We grabbed coffee, Americano, fresh beans, and you were chatting about some sort of female synchronicity but I wasn't listening. The rains came down and I was thinking about Edward Thomas and wondered what trees he had seen when he made love on Wimbledon Common to a wife who could not hold onto him. 'Was yours the face that launched a thousand ships,' you joked, your mouth full of muesli and milk. But I couldn't forget that tree, once remembered. How I had once been in another bed. Your mobile went. You were saying, 'You have somebody really on the edge of something,' to who knows who. I took out the mirror, the one you gave me, automatically applied Winterberry, saw the signs: the last one please turn off the lights. Made to go. I know – we will meet soon. They've planted a new sapling in the street outside the place I live now, just a few buds. Looking to the North Star, rooted in litter. From your window, the tree is bone but holds birds. From mine, no birds can be seen. And on the Launceston road, children grown, the maple is in blossom.

THAT SAME SEA

ADRIAN MARKLE

WE SAT on the first-floor balcony of the holiday let that looked down over the village from the hill on the east. I looked south, to the sea, and sometimes back east, towards home. She looked west, over the village, maybe hunting among the rooftops for the house she'd grown up in.

She had tea and I had coffee. Neither of us ate. I still felt delicate, and it was too late now for breakfast anyway. I didn't think the coffee was that great, but I was still mossy-tongued from the night before. I squinted against the sun splashing off the water, still distant but coming in, she'd assured me. She always talked about how suddenly the tide came in here. But for the moment, the boats in the little harbour all lay awkwardly on their sides in the sand, frayed green ropes trailing off limply to wherever. I picked up the paper to shield my eyes.

The front page of the newspaper showed a picture of Brighton Beach, packed shoulder to shoulder with pale, British beachgoers. 'Millions Flock to Brighton to Escape Summer Heatwave,' it said.

'They should just come here,' I said. The little village, the one she'd grown up in, Gorran Haven, was busy with tourists – like myself, I suppose – but not 'millions' busy.

'They don't know,' she said.

'What don't they know?'

'About this. Not really. God's own country. But people don't understand the difference. This is a nice place. A really nice place. But they just see a beach.'

I was surprised by how much she seemed to care for this village, how quickly her old accent was reasserting itself. She never talked about home much, but as soon as we'd booked this weekend she seemed to grow more impassioned about it with each passing week.

'Why not?' I asked.

'Because they're incomers.'

'Like me.'

'Like you.' She winked.

'You're enjoying this.'

'I am. I've had years of you teasing me about not knowing this or that about the city, not knowing the best route on the tube. Now it's your turn to be a little out of place. But it's okay. You're with me.'

'You're not exactly a local yourself any more.'

'Shush. It doesn't leave you. And I'm local enough to know where the good beach is.'

We stood and collected our kit from the foot of the bed and walked past the main beach, jammed with tourists and their tents and chairs and windbreaks and all sorts of other beach furniture, and off up the narrow dirt path that wound its way along the coast, up and over one of the two tall hills that penned in her little village.

The path was uneven and hard, like concrete, and I struggled at first, but she was surefooted, and soon I was hurrying to catch up.

'Good to be back?' I called, hoping to slow her. It worked. We'd got in the night before and then immediately drank too much. Today was her first real day here in years.

She answered with a grunting noise that I couldn't decipher and we continued on in the quiet, slower now – her initial enthusiasm seemingly lessened – up the path.

We crested the hill, and the wind hit us in a way that I had not been prepared for. It didn't get windy like that in the city; it didn't have time to build up speed. She stretched out her arms to feel it blow across her bare skin. Her long black hair lit up and tore and twisted wild in the wind, tangling and untangling. I felt like I could already see that copper rising, that shade that came out in her hair with enough sun, and the pink that rose on her cheeks – even though our holiday was only just a few hours old. She wore the weather on her skin. It got into her and stayed long after any evidence of good weather would have faded from me.

After she'd had her fill, she turned and set off again, me trailing quite contentedly behind. The great rolling hills of close-cropped grass were to our right, and to our left was a steep-then-vertical drop off to the sea.

'It's gorse.' She pointed to some yellow-flowered bushes that grew abundantly between us and the sea. 'Rose is Cornish for gorse, so this is what the Roseland means.'

'Oh. I'd have preferred actual roses.'

'Quiet. This place is magical. Those are ferns,' she said. 'Fiddlehead ferns, maybe.'

She knew I liked hearing things like this. The ferns grew thick, carpet-like, a woven green mass that obscured the actual solid footing of the hill. It was just us, and then the ferns, and then the sea.

'And that's cow parsley,' she said. It grew tall, taller than her in some cases, and its stalks held up little umbrellas of white flowers. 'Sheep go crazy for it.'

'Sheep?'

'Yeah, sheep. Look, they've grazed down the field on the other side of us.'

'Can I see one?'

'I don't know.' She laughed. 'Can you?'

'I mean, I've never actually seen one before, up close.'

She shook her head. 'City folk.'

'Last week you drank a latte out of an avocado, and you've taken your cat to yoga.'

She shrugged. 'Got to do something to make city life bearable.'

I leaned over and reached out for a burst of the flowers of the cow parsley, to get it for her, to pin it in her hair, but she followed my gaze and slapped the back of my hand.

'Don't,' she said. 'It'll only die if you pick it. Besides, don't lean off the path like that. Dangerous.'

We continued on around the head, with her still naming things occasionally – foxglove, blackberry brambles, ivy – until the path split, and we took the one that angled down to a long, fat curve of pebbled beach, dramatically walled in on either side by two spits of rocky headland, and populated by only a few other couples. Good to be an insider. Fuck Brighton.

'Vault Beach,' she said.

The path we did not take continued up along the edge of the hill, eventually passing, I now saw, a field that had sheep in it, and a part of me wished we'd gone that way.

We dropped our things and kicked off our sandals way, way back on the beach. When the tide comes in, it comes in like a flash, she'd said. Our things would be washed away before we even knew we were in danger of losing them.

By the time our toes touched the sand, the air was hot. I was already sweating and probably starting to burn. Had to be well over twenty degrees. We walked out, but not straight out, instead tracing the headland in and over and around the rocks, to which our access was granted by the still-absent tide. It had come in only so much as to wet our feet and ankles.

'It's the same.' She beamed. 'It's all the same as I remember.'

'What's the sound?' I asked. I loved to see her smile like that, but there was something echoing down the little cliff, a deep growl and a lighter, grinding, metallic rattle that made me nervous.

She cocked her head.

'Chain harrow.'

I nodded. I had no idea what she was talking about, but I nodded.

'A farmer's driving round somewhere on a quad bike, towing a net of chain that turns over the soil.'

I nodded again.

'Now hurry up. I'm going to show you something, if you'll move your lazy ass!'

She ran off and I chased after and we clambered about in the shade cast by the headland, tracing, down there on the sand, roughly the same path that continued along the cliff above us.

The water was knee high now, and I splashed seawater at her as she forged ahead, the droplets falling and disappearing in her wake without her ever knowing they'd been there.

'Look,' she said, and I hurried to catch up. 'The grotto!' I could hear the memories coming back to her. She pointed to a cleft in the cliff face and turned into it. I followed her. We walked through the rock where it parted like tied-back curtains. The base of the grotto was higher than the beach we'd come from, and we were soon less than ankle deep again, spraying cloudy, silty water about us with each step.

In the recess stood a sheep, a young one, white wool and white face. It was near motionless and didn't react to us at all.

We sidled up to the sheep, not wanting to spook it. Though it must have been able to hear the splash of our steps, it didn't run. Didn't even so much as look, just stood, waiting.

'Is this …?' I started to ask.

'No, not normal at all,' she said, and she moved toward it, then reached back and grabbed my hand and we approached together. It was cold in there.

I felt nervous as I approached, like I was imposing.

I reached out. Its fleece was much softer than I'd imagined, not coarse or oily as I'd expected, though dirty and caked with sand. The animal was small, mostly leg. Maybe still a lamb, yet. It turned its head ever so slightly in to my hand, I thought, when I scratched between its ears, but otherwise gave little response.

Its eyes were glassy. I took my hand away, and it didn't seem to notice.

'Come and look,' she said.

She brushed some of the red-tinged wool away from its rear haunch. The sheep flinched a little, but otherwise didn't move. There was blood in its fleece, and skin carved smoothly from its hip, all the way down its leg, as if it had been peeled back by a cleaver. The muscle, deep red and glistening, was dirty and sandy as well.

And then I realised that the stones beneath my feet and behind me were darkened, blood-slicked. The bleeding seemed to have stopped now, but the evidence of it was ample, and the amount of it slowly weeping down through the ground was probably significant.

She too had noticed, had picked up her feet to see the crimson dotting her soles.

I craned my neck up the dizzying distance to the top of the cliff.

'Must have fallen going after the … whatever. Parsley,' I said. 'What do we do?'

'I … don't know,' she said. The confidence that had flown her around the coast path seemed to have disappeared, and she seemed as surprised by that as I was. Her voice was quieter now. 'Go and get someone, I suppose? They'll know what to do in the village. Or at least, they'll know someone who does. We could get that guy, the one driving the quad bike?'

I scratched the sheep behind the ear again, and again it sort of nudged into me, its tongue drooping slightly from its mouth.

'Let's hurry, though, yeah?' I said.

'Yeah.'

'How long do you think we have?' I asked, glancing at the incoming tide.

'I don't know,' she said. 'It comes in all at once. How high do you think it comes up in here?'

Inside of the recess, I saw a clear line drawn on the rocks up above our heads, smooth and dark, where the water reached when the tide came in.

'Too high. I … I could run?'

'No,' she said.

The tide didn't appear to be coming in quickly, but it was.

'What should we do?' I asked. 'What should we do?' I was an outsider, an incomer, an emmet, and I was left frozen by that feeling – my hand slapped away from the cow parsley.

And for a second it seemed she felt the same way, and we stood dumbly, the three of us, and waited.

The sun shone down into the crevice and the tide rose up from below, the water licking now at the bottom of her cut-off jeans and the sheep's belly.

She stooped, wrapped her arms around all four of its young legs, hesitated, and then stood. The sheep, which had been still this whole time, came alive the second the exposed flesh of its leg, made cold by the sea breeze, pressed against her lightly-freckled shoulder and painted it a dark red.

I was stunned by her boldness, and if the young sheep's sudden struggling, the kicking of its legs to break free, hadn't caused it to start slipping from her grasp, I might have just stood, witnessing, until she was gone.

But instead I stepped forward and took the animal from her, its kicking easier for me to manage, even as it began to bleed again with each frantic pump of its leg, the blood sliding slow down the inside of my arm, the side of my chest. It screamed at first too, a plaintive, cracking baa that sounded both completely alien and far too human.

With the water now suddenly up past our knees, and then almost to our hips, it was a lot harder to walk in to the shore than it had been to walk out.

Then the lamb began to calm, and quieten, and by the time we rounded the corner to set eyes on the beach, it had ceased most of its protests save for the occasional, weakening kick, and moved no more than it had when we'd first seen it.

'Do you think it'll be okay?' she asked.

I kept walking.

The few people on the shore stood still and watched us walk in, like they were expecting us. I heard someone shout something, but I couldn't make out what it was. I worried they'd think we were somehow responsible. I worried that we somehow were, that we'd made ourselves responsible for this by getting involved, especially as I now wore the red evidence of my interference down my side, blood that would not have been lost if we had left the lamb alone.

But she pressed on, forging through the rising tide, and I followed, easier, in her wake.

Eventually, the water began to fall lower and lower on our legs, and then we were on what remained of the beach. We stood there not knowing what to do next for maybe seconds or maybe minutes. Nothing seemed to move. And then someone was walking across the beach out to meet us. Very young. Still a boy. He had a black, Cornish flag T-shirt with the sleeves ripped off, dirty jeans, and work boots with worn tongues that hung away from them like from the mouths of dying animals. His hair was the colour of hay, sun-bleached and coarsened by the salt wind, and his cheeks were crimson, chapped.

''Ere,' he said, and held out his arms. He was Cornish, at least, which I felt made him an authority. 'Give 'e 'ere.'

So I surrendered the sheep, and the boy held it with a practised ease, and then he placed it gently on the back of his quad bike and fastened it firmly down with some straps and rode off the beach and away up the hill. We stood and watched until the bike crested the hill and passed out of view.

We packed up our things and held them at arm's length, so as not to bloody them, and headed back up the path. It was still sunny out. Still twenty-five degrees. Still a beautiful day.

We showered for a long time back at the holiday let, and sat out on the balcony. I looked over the quiet village – the white buildings, ashy streets and ruddy brown stone walls occasionally disturbed by a flash of colour, the orange of a child's inflatable boat, the yellow of a snorkel, or the sky blue of a beach towel some other tourist was carrying back contentedly from the main beach.

'Anywhere else you wanted to take me today?' I asked.

She shook her head. She got up, and leaned over the balcony a while, and shook her head again. She walked back inside, and the door closed behind her.

HOME BETWEEN SEA AND STONE

TIM MARTINDALE

IRON ON iron, iron on stone. Arthur's gaze wanders to his father working – his hammer rising and falling as he chips away at the lump of granite before him, worn creases moving in his leather apron. Sharp flakes of stone fly off and make a bid for freedom out of the open shed. An old acrid smell like gunpowder lingers in the air.

Arthur is supposed to be on magpie duty. The swallows have arrived and made their nest under the corrugated metal roof of one of the empty masons' huts. They dart in and out with food for the just-hatched chicks, scything low over the meadow beside the yard, catching flies on the wing. It's a hot, humid day in July and long grasses and wild flowers nod against heavy dark clouds, even as the sun bathes the quarry in soft clear light; it glints off the quartz in the granite stacked in piles around the yard, the spray of water from the saw and the blue sea beyond. Occasionally Arthur sees his father look up as if he were admiring the queer beauty of it all. He thinks of winters here, when the wind howls through the yard, perched as it is on the edge of a deep quarry, the quarry's mouth yawning out to sea and the gusting breath roaring out of it.

Arthur sits on the edge of a crate of stone slabs, legs dangling, catapult aimed across the yard, ready to defend the remaining swallows from the clutches of the hated magpies. They grabbed two from the nest last week.

'They haven't flown all the way here just to have their young pinched by some bloody thievin' robber birds,' his father had declared one day, laying a big hand on Arthur's shoulder and handing him the catapult.

Days are long in the quarry in summertime. In wintertime Arthur is busy keeping the fires burning that warm the masons in their draughty sheds. Weeks slip by and he feels he's hardly thought about anything much at all. But, watching his father, he wonders if he'll grow old and stiff there, hammering away day after day till he goes grey, hard and cold like granite.

Out of the corner of his eye Arthur spies a kestrel hovering out over the quarry. Drawn to the edge, he leans ever so gently into the wind, feeling the gulf in front of him, and imagines himself being lifted with an upward draught and, like a feather, being borne out to sea. Looking out to where ships lie at anchor in the bay, he loses himself for a moment amongst the swaying masts.

'Think you can fly, quarry boy?' Startled, he almost loses his balance, but bony fingers grip his arm and pull him back. Michael. Arthur isn't yet sure if he is friend or foe. There is something dangerous about him.

The sun had barely risen that same morning when Arthur ran into Michael for the first time. He had climbed down the cliff to the beach to go wrecking early before work. The quarry was like a beast with a huge stomach, mouth agape to the sea. It needed to be fed a lot. The cutting saws, the pumps to keep the water at bay, the forge to keep the tools sharp, the fires to keep the men warm, all ate up coal. Then there was the timber: props for tunnelling and blasting, rollers for hauling on, struts for resting the stone on whilst the masons worked. Arthur asked his grandfather once, 'How come God gave us Cornish so much sea to sail on and no trees to build boats with?'

'If God gave us everything we needed there'd be no reason setting sail in the first place,' was his grandfather's matter-of-fact reply.

Now and again a shipload of coal arrived from Wales, or timber from Norway, but mostly the quarry consumed wreckage. A lump of coal as big as his father's fist earned Arthur five shillings, a plank of wood twenty. Not that it was always easy getting hold of it. There was competition on the beach, especially after a big storm. Fights broke out sometimes. Arthur saw Will Carne, the smithy's son, come back with a black eye once. Arthur had heard stories of Michael, who lived down on the beach, an upturned fishing boat for a house. Gone in the head, they said. Lost his father and brothers all in one night when their fishing boat was wrecked. Mother ended up in the workhouse. He was tall and gangly but stronger than he looked from hauling wreck all day long. He'd trade a pot or a plank for a fish or a knife or anything else he needed to survive.

A big piece of timber bobbing about on the tide had caught Arthur's eye. He stopped and had a quick look around. He wasn't alone. Michael was crouched on a rock at the sea's edge, knife in hand. He'd been cleaning out limpet shells for breakfast. He saw Arthur; they both glanced at the wood. Suddenly Michael leapt onto the sand and then he was running. Arthur's head was screaming to get out of there, but he found himself running hard for it too. And he could really run. He reached it first and threw himself onto the wood. With a great heave, he pulled it out of the water. Michael was on him in a heartbeat. Still knee-deep in the shallows, Arthur started to swing and jab the plank wildly.

'Come any nearer and I'll bash yer head in,' he yelled, his voice more high-pitched than he intended. Michael eyeballed him, not saying anything. A long time seemed to pass. Eventually he lowered the knife, closed it deftly with one hand and dropped it into a pocket in trousers which didn't quite reach his ankles. Feeling foolish, Arthur lowered the plank.

'What's yer name, crazy boy?'

'Arthur Trewin.'

Michael nodded. 'S'pose I be letting you keep that plank this time, but next time you come wrecking in my patch, I swear I'll kill you.'

'You aren't owning this beach,' Arthur blurted out. He was trying hard to show he wasn't afraid, but his voice and arms were shaking. Michael's eyes narrowed.

'Where you from?'

'Mousehole.'

'Fisherman?'

'Quarryman,' replied Arthur, puffing his chest out.

'How old are you?'

'Fourteen.'

Michael didn't look convinced. 'Don't you want to go to sea?' he said darkly, spitting on the sand.

Arthur shrugged. His mouth went dry and his voice caught. 'Father's a quarryman and we lost Uncle to the deep and you know …'

Michael's face was turned to the sea but Arthur saw a flicker of pain cross it.

'Well, she'll get you one way or another.' With that Michael was off, leaping across the rocks and disappearing around the point under the cliffs.

Arthur gazed after him for a while before his eyes were drawn to the fishing boats making their way out to the grounds, the sun climbing up behind them, sea and sky turning black to blue like a bruise. With a heavy heart he began his climb up the cliff to the quarry, clasping his hard-won wreck.

*

'You idiot, I could have fallen,' cries Arthur, shrugging Michael's bony grip off and moving away from the quarry edge. 'What you doing up here anyway?'

Michael scowls, stands back to look Arthur up and down and takes a long drag on a roll of smouldering tobacco.

'How can you stand it? Working yer guts out all day, making some quarry-owner rich?'

'It's good enough for Father.'

'Then he's a fool, too.'

'You take that back,' Arthur shouts, fists clenched. He takes a step towards Michael then hears his father banging on the wall of his shed. Poking his head round he sees the foreman striding up the yard, face turning scarlet about a late order.

'Better make yourself and your friend scarce for a bit,' warns his father. 'Foreman's on the warpath.'

'Quick, this way,' Arthur hisses to Michael, as he disappears over the edge and down the quarry face. 'Mind your bloody step. Some of the rungs are rusted out.'

They climb down the ladders until they land on the first ledge, all overgrown with fern and gorse, made when the quarrymen blasted out huge blocks the size of houses.

'That's a peregrine's nest.' Arthur points to a mess of congealed blood, feathers and guano. 'You can see the bones of its last kill.' Michael nods, quiet and serious. Arthur's gaining the upper hand. He's in his territory now. They scurry down the last set of ladders and jump into the long grass below.

The quarry's been like home for Arthur since his mother died of cholera. Eseld was her name. Arthur's father carved her stone himself, chiselled a bird under her name, a chough; she had loved to watch them on the sea cliffs. Now, in the summer when it's warm and there's not much work to keep Arthur occupied, Father often sends him off to explore the quarry workings. Sometimes Arthur climbs down these ladders to go swimming, even though the quarry bottoms are dark and cold and no one knows how deep.

Arthur and Michael stare into the inky depths.

'Do you believe in mermaids?' asks Arthur. Michael nods. Something strange has come over him and he stares transfixed.

'They say the quarrymen dug too deep and they reached caves that run underground to the sea and it's in these caves that the sea spirits live. That's where the dead go,' Arthur confides as if passing on a secret. His grandmother told him that, after his mother was taken.

'Dare you to swim.'

Michael hesitates.

'Coward.'

Michael starts to tear off his clothes and Arthur joins him. 'Last one in's a rotten egg!'

They're laughing now, with a mixture of fear and excitement. Their naked bodies are white as pearls in the black water, as quarry dust, dirt and sand fall away from them.

It is a two-mile walk home along the coast path. Arthur walks alongside his father as he does every day. The day is still warm and the sky is hanging heavy over the sea, like a big rain is coming. Sweat is running down his father's face in rivulets, and Arthur thinks for a moment that his father's crying, but he hasn't ever seen him cry, even after his mother went.

They are often quiet and weary but today Arthur chatters away about Michael – how he lives in a boat on the beach, catches rabbits and gathers mussels for his tea, how he swims like a fish and how he lost his father and then his mother went away. Arthur sees his father grow sad and distant then, so to distract him he asks if he can take Michael some vegetables from the garden – his teeth and gums are no good – and can he go and camp out under the boat? His father lays his hand on his shoulder and says gently, 'Not tonight, boy. I reckon there's a storm brewin', don't you? Another day, when the weather be fine.'

From the path Arthur can see the fishing pack rounding Carn-du on the way home from the western fishing grounds. They look so free to him, like a flock of wild geese, with rusty brown lug-sails full of wind and grace. Yet nothing makes Arthur's heart sing more than the sight of the three-mast barques and the great tall ships returning from the Mediterranean or the Americas. Now, one of those great leviathans appears, making fast headway riding a sou'westerly and so he breaks into a run and races the ship home. He leaps with giant steps over great lumps of granite strewing the path. The smell of summer gorse fills his nostrils and cormorants swoop low over the rocks. Tiny vegetable plots and gardens on the cliff edge pass by in a blur.

As he draws round the point, stops to catch his breath and let his father catch up, his heart lifts again, as it always does coming home. He gazes down onto the village nestled snug in the cove, smoke curling up from the houses into a dusky blue sky, fishing boats packed tightly in the tiny harbour, men's voices rising on the still evening air, as fish are being unloaded, sails furled, nets strung out to dry. Arthur and his father come down the hill past the row of old boys sitting out in their sea caps, catching the last of the sun.

His father turns his back on the sea to go into the cottage. Arthur pauses, torn between thinking he should keep his father company and help in the garden and wanting to go and see what the boats have brought in. With a nod and a knowing smile, his father says, 'You go on now, son, but make sure you're home before the weather breaks.'

Down on the quay a strong arm hoists him up onto the deck of the Our Boys, amidst boxes of cod, sole, turbot, ray, ling and gleaming silver mackerel. Boys leap from boat to boat, eager to swap stories and compare catches. A friend of Arthur's bounds up to him saying they'd come close to a French privateer on the way home and one of the navy ships fired warning cannon and escorted the Our Boys as far as Plymouth.

A box is thrust into Arthur's hands to pass down to the quay. Someone starts to sing and the song passes from boat to boat, rising like a sea swell. The womenfolk are leaning over the railings calling and counting out the crews – sons, husbands, and fathers. The crews are tight and disciplined and they proudly unload the boxes, clean the deck, coil the ropes, even tie extra knots, smirking to one another, enjoying making their sweethearts wait. One of the seasoned deckhands elbows Arthur in the ribs and points to where dark clouds are gathering out in the bay.

'That storm will have every man and woman warming their drunken cockles in bed before long, you mark my words, boy,' he says with a wink. Arthur thinks of Michael then, sheltering under his boat with a hard sea at his back.

When night comes, the rain lashes Arthur's window as he lies curled in bed. The candle flickers in the draught and the wind claws to get in. He remembers how his mother used to sing to him at night. She comes to him again now, through a fog of drowsiness.

'Can't you sleep?' she says, treading softly on small bare feet. She climbs in, pulls him close to her warm body, and sweeps the hair from his hot brow.

'Will you sing the knight song?' Arthur asks his mother. It's an old English song she used to sing to him at night. The words of the last chorus swim through Arthur's half-slumber.

There's a yellow moon swinging over the sea like a lantern and a boy's sleeping face. A boy alone, with an upturned fishing boat for a home, the wind howling and the sea raging around him.

THE HOPE OF RECOVERY

ELAINE RUTH WHITE

THE JUNE sun fizzed then dissolved as the sea rushed over her face.

Suspended for a moment in that sliver of space between exhilaration and anxiety, an unfamiliar thought washed through her mind. This time, would she come back?

She should not have been going alone. She knew that. So did the Porthoustock fisherman she'd persuaded to take her.

He'd no love of divers, that was for sure. More than once, just for sport, they'd cut the orange-buoyed ropes securing his costly lobster pots, pots he'd never get to retrieve. Sometimes they'd take the buoys as trophies. Or to decorate their gardens. Other times, believing themselves noble saviours, they would release his catch of lobster and crab, making it that much harder to put food on the table through the winter months. The £150 plus fuel costs she'd offered him 'righted some wrongs', he'd said. But she knew from the deepening sun-cuts in his face that, despite the wrongs and the money she offered, his agreement was not without conscience.

She carried out a solo buddy check, silently mouthing the mantra designed to keep her safe: BWRAF – buoyancy, weights, releases, air, final OK. She mentally noted the presence of the sharp, serrated knife strapped to her calf in case she became entangled in abandoned fishing net. She slid her left hand down her right shoulder strap, checking the security of the underwater camera clipped to the D-ring on her buoyancy jacket and the torch that would help her find what she was looking for. Then, placing the regulator in her mouth, she crossed her arms over her chest and let the weight of her air tank tip her backward from where she sat precariously on the side of the boat. And she fell.

Breaking back through the surface, as she'd done a thousand times before, she touched the tip of her right index finger to the tip of her thumb, and made the familiar OK signal to the boatman.

'Forty minutes,' he warned.

She signalled OK again, before giving a thumbs down – the signal for descent – and slowly let the air out of her buoyancy jacket, slipping under the water, leaving only pools of exhaled breath on the surface.

She loved this place.

Shore diving had long been banned from Porthallow Beach – Pralla to the locals – the result of destructive, disruptive behaviour by groups of loutish divers. Boats were now the only, more expensive, option to scuba-dive these waters. But it had always been worth it.

Porthallow Cove was sheltered from westerlies and in any case, today saw nothing more than a gentle force 2, meaning no white horses racing toward the shore. Nevertheless, it didn't do to forget the cove was perilously close to Manacles Reef, with its ferocious currents and gigantic submerged rocks that had bitten their way into many a ship's hull.

Diving the Manacles, a badge of honour for many, was restricted to slack water, that hour between the ebb and flow of the tide when the sea idled before roaring back into life. Only a fool would push their luck too far. But it happened, and the Manacles had taken many a life. Sailors. Fishermen. Travellers. The unwise. The unlucky. Churchyards on the peninsula testified to the tragedies, as well as the courage of the Cornish men and women who'd risked their lives trying to save passengers and crew alike. Many were saved, but many more perished, like those lying cradled in one grave in St Keverne, its monumental granite headstone bearing the stark word: Mohegan. But none of this was on her mind now, as looking down she gasped at the emerging beauty. It was just as it had always been, like diving an aquarium.

Porthallow Reef, at little more than ten metres depth, and on such a bright day, was crystal clear. Scattered below, littering the quartz-glittered granite, sparkling like jewels in the penetrating sunlight, were round white sea urchins, with shells so much lovelier in life than dried out in baskets outside souvenir shops. And purple snakelocks anemones, their sting the reason she always wore lightweight neoprene gloves, even when the water temperature was balmy, for Cornwall, at 18°C. Long-legged spider crabs clambered like alien creatures over the sand and silt seabed. Camouflaged cuttlefish scuttled and merged into the tall swaying kelp that was furred with plankton. Outlines of flatfish were visible in the sand beneath which they hid. Tiny velvet swimming crabs danced on their rear legs, waving their claws and daring the world to take them on. Transparent shrimps flitted round dark mouths of inlets where conger eels lurked. Dogfish darted in and around. Silvered mackerel, wrasse, multi-coloured cuckoo fish – so much life …

Her throat tightened.

She checked her air gauge and watch. Six minutes already gone. Releasing more air from her jacket she completed her descent, hovering in neutral buoyancy two metres from the seabed. At this depth it was shallow enough for her air to last a full forty minutes, giving her a safety margin before the sea began to suck back through the reef. Kicking gently with her right fin, she turned her upper body to the left and began to track her intended route.

Except for the seasons, the terrain here did not change much, not even after a storm. That was something they'd both loved: revisiting familiar territory, knowing which nooks were home to a crab or lobster, which shelves or gullies housed a conger eel. The natural world seemed timeless. Only the wrecks would change, as the salt water eroded their twisted metal skins, sculpting them less over decades.

The sea around Cornwall had provided ample scope for one of their favourite arguments: where were the best dive sites? They'd dived the globe together. Thailand. Egypt. Mexico. Australia. Sri Lanka. But always they'd come home to these waters, where visibility was never as good, wildlife never as colourful, nor water temperatures something to relish. But there was always something magical about the waters off the Lizard. Always something to bring back.

Nothing made a dive more special than discovering 'treasure': a John Dory photographed on a night dive, its startled spines caught large in the torchlight, a discarded urchin shell from a drift dive out from Penzance, a piece of clay pipe from a German U-boat off Pendennis headland. But the best things they brought back were the stories.

The one they'd loved and laughed over most often was their find on the wreck of the SS Volnay, a merchant ship lying off Porthallow. Destroyed in 1917 by a German mine, she'd carried, amongst other things, munitions – many shells and detonators remaining live despite almost a century submerged.

It was usual for divers to be dropped onto the wreck's bow, or more often, onto what remained of her boilers. On one dive they'd found a perfectly intact lump of coal that had been intended to fire her engines. It was the size of a very large house brick, and looked like a diamond-shaped bar of black soap, the date of cutting and manufacturer's name in relief on its face. Delighted with their find, they'd taken it back to the cottage they shared in an out-of-the-way hamlet near Cadgwith and left it to dry. That winter, short of cash and coal for their ancient Cornish range, they'd lit newspaper and wood from an old dining chair. Then, not expecting to succeed, placed the salvaged coal into the flames.

Within seconds it had burst into life, flaring as if enraged it had ever been lost, left for so long, never fulfilling its purpose. She'd marvelled at its defiant spirit, arguing it proved the old adage 'where there's life there's hope', but Sarah had laughed, roundly mocking her, saying she was full of romantic nonsense: more likely it was traces of cordite that had become welded into the side of the coal when the ship went down.

They'd loved to find 'treasure', never knowingly destroying anything in the process, unlike those who used explosives to rip apart the bodies of the wrecks, desecrating what were often war graves, looting whatever they could find. When she dived with Sarah, they took nothing more than the discarded or inadvertently dropped. Watches were a common find, as were sunglasses and bottles and once, lying in the barest patch of sand surrounded by a group of bemused hermit crabs, a sealed case stuffed with packs of white powder, dropped in haste, no doubt, at the sight of an approaching coastguard vessel.

The seabed held the remnants of so many lives. For that reason, wreck dives were the most special. She understood the desire to retrieve something, return something that had been taken away; she understood the compulsion to restore the balance, right the unfairness. Sometimes the simplest piece of broken cup or plate could feel like the most precious find, when it came with the knowledge that at some point in the distant past, a hand had held it, or lips sipped from it. Whether because of the lives attached to them, or the submerged worlds they'd become, wrecks held a special magic.

Meghan shook loose the memories and began to move slowly, carefully, so her fin tips didn't disturb the sand and silt – a sure way to destroy the visibility. She knew why she was there, her purpose had been firm in her mind from the minute she'd made the decision, but just for a moment, she wanted to revisit everything she'd seen five years ago on their first dive together. She wanted to recapture the awe, the magic, their whole falling in love with the place.

She believed she would remember the route instinctively, that despite the years that had passed she would know exactly where she was heading, how long it would take. As she focused on navigating her way through the thick kelp, a sudden shadow passed overhead, momentarily blocking the light. She looked up sharply, her breath quickening, briefly using her air more rapidly. She squinted against the light, trying to make out the strange silhouette above her, not recognising its shape. Then she gasped. It was a sunfish. Usually found in the tropics, she knew the odd, disc-shaped creature visited these waters, but she'd never seen one. They were a marvel. Female sunfish could lay more eggs than any other vertebrate in the world – up to 300 million each season – a massive vessel of potential life.

Forgetting everything else, she turned to stay in its shadow, grasping for the carabiner clip of the camera attached to the D-ring on her buoyancy jacket. As the sunfish began to move beyond her, she finned harder, thankful the waters were giving less resistance than they might if she were swimming against an onshore current. But despite her efforts, the sunfish moved out of sight. Disappointment raked briefly before she instinctively checked her air gauge and watch; she had thirty minutes of air left if she remained at a depth of twelve metres, but her depth gauge indicated she was in deeper water – sixteen metres. Her trajectory had been to travel north-east to south-west from the boat. But the distraction of the sunfish meant she had changed direction. Porthallow Cove was now behind her and New York, if she kept going for 3,000 miles, in front. Her destination was little more than a couple of hundred feet from where the boat had dropped her and she'd been confident she could navigate by terrain from the route they'd always taken. But, no longer on that route, she'd lost her way.

She turned a full 360 degrees, but could spot nothing familiar. The waters at her new depth had grown darker, more turbid, taking on a gloomy, grey-blue tinge. The outlines of the rocks that had given such definition before were now much less distinct. There was less colour. Less life. She checked her depth gauge again: eighteen metres now. Her breath came faster, filling her lungs and using air more quickly. With increased depth came increased atmospheric pressure and the neoprene of her suit began to compress, causing the fin on her right foot to loosen and try to break free. She grasped at the strap, pulling it tighter, at the same time remembering angry words from the past.

'I don't care,' Sarah had spat, 'how good a metaphor it is, or its place in feminist literature; a fin is a fin, not a flipper! Flipper's a dolphin! 'Diving into a Wreck'? I doubt the woman ever dived in her life!'

'It's Diving into the Wreck. Maybe get your facts straight before you have a go about stuff beyond your limited comprehension,' Meghan had retorted, grateful the poet hadn't committed the ultimate sin of referring to a diving mask as 'goggles'.

'A wreck, the wreck. Whatever.'

It was how they used to fight. With words aimed at soft but well-known targets. Words that were sometimes clever, sometimes cruel, and usually stirred by something stupid. For the past two years, Meghan had lain awake at night regretting every harsh word ever spoken between them.

At the time it had driven her mad, the way Sarah fixated on one detail, one notion, one word, then would rant intransigently. Most times Meghan had been able to switch off to it, but not about that; she loved Adrienne Rich's poems and that one particularly meant something to her beyond the interpretations. She'd read it to Sarah, wanting to share an intimacy, wanting her to find the same depth in the piece.

But Sarah never got it, couldn't see beyond the concrete. Or refused to. Instead, she'd focused on that one small detail and exposed it mercilessly. It was the same when Sarah got sick, that picking at words.

'Necrotising fasciitis eats. Leprosy eats. This thing doesn't eat. It grows. It spreads. It colonises. It doesn't eat.'

That was her way of dealing with things. Get angry. Yell. Fight. But despite the fight, Sarah sank into the cancer, as it grew and it spread and it colonised.

Meghan blinked away the past, as the sea around her became a cold, dark violet that edged an uncompromising blackness. Her unplanned descent continued. With increased depth, each lungful of air took more from her tank than she'd allowed for. As she sank, she felt the weight of the lead around her waist, the steel tank on her back. As if in a dream, her left hand reached for the inflator valve on her buoyancy jacket that would lift her from the deepening waters. But she didn't press it. She hovered there, unmoving, staring into the gloom. So easy, she thought, it would be so easy now. The weight would keep her down. The current would take her deeper, further out; thirty, forty metres. They'd never find her. It would spare them the funeral at least, that grotesque farce where nothing of a life is truly revealed. Nothing of the person is really there.

Salt water stung her eyes. Instinctively she pressed the heel of her hand to the top rim of her mask and tilted her head; breathing out through her nose to clear her mask of what her training led her to believe was seawater. But it wasn't the sea that had leaked in, and her vision continued to blur until she could no longer make out her surroundings. There were no shapes. No colour.

But there was a sound, faint and distant, but distinct. It sounded like a bell.

There'd been stories of a bell being heard by divers when they visited the Manacles Reef. It was said to be that of the SS Mohegan, which sank on only her second voyage. She'd hit the Manacles Reef on 14 October 1898 with the loss of 106 of the 197 on board. The wreck of the Mohegan lay twenty-four metres down, gripped in the massive jaws of rock pinnacles, starkly covered in spongy, white dead man's fingers.

Logic should have told her the sound could not be a bell. More like it was the creeping effect of nitrogen narcosis, a side effect of breathing compressed air at depth. No bell would ring down here. But she was no longer in a place where logic worked well for her.

She strained to hear, to judge its distance. Sound travels much faster through water than air, making it hard to judge direction. As she swam, the light continued to fade with her increase in depth. She heard it again. Straight ahead. Or was it to the right?

At once she felt tired. And heavy. It felt as if the weight was in her heart, not in the belt around her waist. She closed her eyes. She could sleep now. She could just drift away and sleep.

Sleep had not come easily since she'd first felt the lump in Sarah's breast. They'd agreed it was probably nothing, but best to get it checked. Sarah, at only thirty, had always behaved as if she were immortal, always being the one who would want to take the biggest risks, make the deeper dives. She'd always been the one to take on the world. Meghan had never been that brave, but Sarah had given her the courage to face most of her fears. And while Sarah turned on the cancer with a warrior-like strength, with the belief that any enemy could be fought, though not necessarily beaten, Meghan had dealt with it the only way she could – by pretending it didn't exist, that it would just go away and everything would be fine. At times she still couldn't bring herself to believe that Sarah was really gone and had been for two years: two years in which Meghan had existed in a fog that sometimes seemed lighter, sometimes darker, but never disappeared.

After the funeral was over and friends had melted back into their own lives, Meghan began to see Sarah everywhere she went. So for weeks she stopped going out. But Sarah filled the cottage and Meghan couldn't bring herself to throw out her clothes and possessions. She was caught between the desire to move on and the delusion that one day Sarah might come back and would be mad as hell if she found her stuff gone.

She'd refused antidepressants, but after the first year, had given in to her doctor's pressure to have grief counselling. She went once, hating to hear her own words as they were reflected back to her, hating to admit that Sarah was gone, hating to reveal her own hopelessness. She'd tried alcohol, once swallowing half a leftover bottle of Sarah's Jack Daniel's, but it had only made her sick. And so she slept. For months, until the sick notes ran out and the anniversary of Sarah's death loomed for a second time. In desperation, she'd gone back to the counsellor who'd suggested she did something positive, significant, to mark the anniversary.

On one of their many dives at Porthallow Cove, they'd found what might have been the signs of a shipwreck. There was precious little of it left, just a few large, very ancient timbers that may have once supported the rigging. There was also a curved beam wedged into a gully. They knew from the growth on the timbers and their condition that it had been there a very long time. On one of their subsequent visits to the site, they'd found a stout, beige, glazed pottery bottle, chipped, but not broken. The bottle had helped them date what they soon convinced themselves was an uncharted, undiscovered wreck – their wreck. Whatever the truth, it didn't really matter to them; for Sarah and Meghan, it was their find, their secret. Many an evening was spent spinning tales of the life of their wreck, who'd sailed her, where she'd been, how she was lost.

They never told a soul about the site and when the counsellor suggested Meghan marked the anniversary by doing something significant, she knew exactly what she would do. She would go there. Alone.

Once the thought had taken root in her mind, it would not go away. Some nights it woke her cold with sweat from fear of what she would have to face. She'd never dived alone. Sarah had been her strength. Goading, encouraging. The fear and desire to run away was overpowering at times, but one thing drove her on. Sarah would be so proud, she told herself. Sarah would be amazed. She wouldn't believe it when Meghan told her. But you can't tell her, a voice said. It's pointless, Sarah will never know. But I'll know, Meghan had told herself, I'll know. And anyway, who knows what Sarah can see, who knows. Maybe she's gone and that's that, but maybe, who knows … No one really knows.

Breaking out of her lethargy, she kicked down, moving her body upward through the water, allowing the air in her buoyancy jacket to expand with the relief of pressure. Checking her compass, she turned back toward the path that should navigate to her destination.

She moved faster through the water now, trading the risk of running out of air against the risk of running out of time before slack water ended and the powerful outgoing tide took over. Ahead of her she saw the edge of a deep channel, its shape seeming distinctive and familiar. She remembered she had to pass a gully to access a narrower channel, and then she would see a line of stones in the seabed, the Seven Sisters they'd named them. The gully was choked with kelp and the camera and torch kept catching. There was no sign of the stones. She was stupid to think nothing would have changed here. Stupid to trust her own memory. She felt the panic start to rise and concentrated on slowing her breath. Switching on her torch, she moved as slowly as she dared, sweeping the light from side to side. There were no stones. She was at the point of no return. She could go back to the boat and safety or continue to search with the remaining minutes of her air in the hope she would find what she was looking for. She went on.

Using her compass, she followed an imaginary line, then turned left into a wide opening with tall rocks at the entrance. Her heart quickened. She thought she recognised the shapes of those rocks, then pushing through the kelp she saw the first of the stones lying on the seabed. Then others. Seven in total. She knew that a few more metres in was their wreck. As she entered the final channel, she saw it, just on the edge of visibility, the place where the timbers stood proud amongst the kelp, the tops of which were being sucked gently offshore as they felt the first turnings of the current. She unclipped her torch to better see her way.

As she finned towards her goal, she became immersed in memories. Her throat ached as a collage of their visits to the place began to unfold. She remembered the times when visibility was so poor they had swum straight into it or past before seeing it. And the time they found it guarded by a very large and very fierce-looking crab they'd named Herman, for no reason at all. And the time they stayed so long searching for more pieces of wreck they had almost run out of air. All these memories and more came back to her until at last the familiar shape loomed out of the kelp and relief flooded through her. It was still there. She raised her torch and the light danced along the beams. And that's when she saw it. Carved into the timbers, into their wreck:

KEVIN
WAS
HERE

She stared in disbelief at the words now scarring the wood, unblinking, until a bitter realisation stung her. Nothing, nothing was sacred. Anything could be taken away. And then it came at her, fast and from nowhere, with its huge black mouth and its rows of relentless, razor-sharp teeth. She howled, letting loose a sound that seemed barely human. She thrashed as hard as she could until the world kaleidoscoped into a thousand bloody, desperate pieces and she span violently upward.

The fisherman stared at the anglerfish lying lifeless on the deck by his feet, a large dive knife sticking out of its spine. He could barely suppress his delight. One of the ugliest creatures in local waters, the anglerfish was better known as monkfish on the menus of the elegant restaurants and gastropubs now lining the Cornish coasts and coves. He knew it would fetch him at least £20 a fillet.

He watched as Meghan dropped her weight belt to the deck. The seawater, draining from her suit and pooling around her feet, was stained with the blood from the bite the anglerfish had inflicted on her hand. She looked different somehow: less fragile, despite her encounter, and he was aware how glad he was she was okay.

'Did you get what you came for?' he asked.

She hesitated, glancing back at the water.

'Yes,' she said. 'I think so.'

I TURN ON MY OWN AXIS

FELICITY NOTLEY

I LAY on my bunk and saw the silhouette of him in the doorway, black against the orange evening sky. Banging of boots on the doorstep. Presently he would come in, but already the anticipation of his smell pervaded the house.

Every night I would awaken just before his return. I could not help but watch as he removed his hair, the flaxen wig that always curled so strangely. I would see how he took a candle and poured liquid into a shallow dish, how he mixed the fluid with a drop of molten wax and painted it on his head.

When he came near, he spoke to me in that gentlemanlike way he had, but the smell of him was like goose fat which had been kept too long, like taffy which had become singed at the edges, like a morsel of food which you raise to your mouth on a fork and have no wish to swallow. You remember how he was; he was much the same on the other side of the world.

One night in early January he took out a letter from his father. Didn't read it, but had it all in his head. He told me of the flooding at the mine and a hundred miners dead. Thought it would be a diversion for me, not the very stopping of my heart. Put the letter down and crossed to the privy.

Only a gentle sigh from him; he cared so little. And in that moment I thought, since I have crossed half a world to come to this new country, which not one of my grandmothers would ever have thought possible, can I not cross half a world to return? Back to the place where the mines lie open, where the snow even now might be clinging to the surface, melting around its curves, dripping into its hollows. Back to where I knew you to be.

The hardest part was waiting, staying indoors day after day, biding my time. I had no expectations, may I just say that? I know you always thought I hoped for too much. Certainly, I had a memory. Everyone has a memory, do they not? Of a night more perfect than most. Grey light, like unpolished silver, right across the moors and a snowfall, soft and even.

On the tenth of February I took my chance. In Oregon they cut down trees, shave their branches, pack them lean and clean like sticks of candy, ship them around the world. There was a vessel sailing for the Spanish coast, docking, I heard, in Falmouth. And although I heard it only once, that was enough. I took my jewellery, for jewels are currency everywhere, and walked out to the harbour.

I have made a discovery in life that most anything is possible if you try it and try it well. I know it was madness, but I took my bundle and walked straight past all those men on the quay in my long skirts and onto the ship. I walked like I was meant to be there and God knew that I was. And once I was on board I made myself invisible.

It's a trick I learned as a child. For if you imagine yourself to be so insignificant, so uninteresting that no one would even want to look at you, you can blend in with your surroundings. You can be a white mouse in a sack of flour.

When we were far out from land, though, I became ill and you almost lost me. I lay in a drench of sweat and could think of nothing but the luxury of a roll over the side of the ship. I longed to fall and be lost in the pit of a wave forever. I hadn't the strength to move. Then my fever left me and my hunger abated and – a curious thing – I found that I could move about the deck freely and no one paid me any mind. I saw that we were in sight of land and in this way I came into Falmouth.

From Falmouth, I walked as my grandmother had done, fifty years before me. My feet did not tire and I had no fear. For three whole days I walked to come back and find you.

And as I walked, what I remembered was this: our last day together. You held a piece of granite in your hand and tapped at the wall by my window. I stepped outside and we walked together, marking a straight line out across the moors. The machinery for once was resting and it was silent in the snow.

You wrapped me in my own coat and you said, 'We will get lost, do you know that? If we walk out into that mist we will lose our way and never return.'

I knew what you meant. That once we were out there, we would not be able to refrain from speaking the truth. We walked together – so sure of the land and so unsure. A gentle slope of white could be the hill we climbed up every day or the opening to a mineshaft long forgotten. The ice we trod on could be the lid of a shallow puddle or it could go on down forever. You told me what you'd heard, how my husband had bought two passages to America. I said I would not travel with him; I wished I did not have to.

The snow covered our tracks, just as you said it would. We ducked into a gentle hollow, held each other closely, slept little. When the mist cleared, the cold was penetrating. I crawled out onto the cusp of a hill and stumbled. I have never seen stars so sharp, so violent in the sky.

I look down now to check the colour where I place my feet. Where it is dazzling white, the snow is firm. Where it holds a hint of shadow, my foot will sink in and come out cooler.

I had expected a grand vista, a worthy homecoming, but instead I am entirely enclosed by mist. I shuffle step after step, not daring to leave the path of footprints, trusting in the tracks of people I don't even know. Just ahead of me is a woman made of snow. Her mouth is twisted and on her head is a bundle of twigs.

I remember the sound of your cough. You coughed always to the same rhythm. You would come to me in the early evenings with your shirt soaked above the level of your nipples. That had been in the last days, when the mines were being failed, when the pumps were too costly to run.

Ahead of me, a granite slab I almost remember. And a lake beyond, so deep the dead could hide – that's what you used to say. The first time we were alone together, you traced your hands over the freckles of my arm. When I remember that, I also remember how silent the cottage was. How the other miners had gone away and it had been just the two of us. I'd turned the key in the lock.

But of course there was no lock. There was no key. It didn't happen like that at all and each time I turn a few degrees on the granite slab, the view shifts and I am more uncertain. It was foolish of me to leave the path, I know, but that's what I've always done. As I turn on my own axis, the view in every direction is exactly the same.

You might have taken me across the surface of the lake. There on the ice you might have lain right beside me. Perhaps I can even remember how it felt: the hardness changing, becoming soft and wet under the back of my head, melting into my hair.

'The surface is an inch thick and hard as iron,' you'd said. 'It won't give.'

But I'd not trusted it and when you rolled onto your side and tried to kiss me, I'd pushed you away. 'We must keep on walking.'

That's what we did. We walked into the rabbit's fur mist.

Snow shoe, snow shoe, snow shoe, my footsteps said, following yours. I am following you still.

THE KISS

PHILIPA ALDOUS

IT WOULDN'T be the first time. She had been kissed before twice. Once by the cousin of a friend. He was fourteen – two years older than her. She hadn't wanted to kiss him. She hadn't even liked him. He had caught her by surprise and held her arms down by her sides as he pressed his mouth briefly against hers. It felt dry … like sand against her lips. A barren kiss. She hated it. She knew she should feel something. She did feel something – that was the worst part – a curling, tender excitement deep inside her, but not for him. She despised him for making her feel something that wasn't his, something he had no right to.

The second kiss was a half kiss. It was just a few weeks after the first, but she was already wiser and better able to take care of herself. The boy lived on her street. This time she had seen it coming and pulled away just as his wet, red lips brushed against hers. She wiped her mouth on the back of her hand. She was tougher now. It didn't touch her.

She knew what kisses had been so far, but she also knew that they could be something different. If Jake kissed her, she knew she would not pull away. If Jake kissed her, she knew the kiss would belong to her.

It was an Indian summer. Everyone said so. She enjoyed the sound of the words. In her mind they conjured a burning orange sky over parched hillsides and the weary tread of footsteps on a dusty track. In fact the sky was the fragile blue of a blackbird's egg and the air was clear and cool over shining dunes. It was mid-September and the holidays had ended. She had been back at school for two weeks, but today was Saturday. The summer visitors were gone. The town was quiet and the empty beach spread out before her under the endless, eggshell sky. She had come down to the shore to scramble over limpet-covered rocks and watch transparent creatures dart in shallow pools.

Each year at this time the beach belonged to her. In this brief snatch of jewel days between the oily, splashing chaos of summer and the weary, drizzle-stained winter, this place was hers. The sand stretched, smooth and unmarked, along the three-mile curve of the bay, waiting for her footprints to disturb it. The sea was quiet and whitely seething, a creature half sleeping, dangerous and drowsy. She walked the wet sand on the very edge of the tide. The tan on her feet was fading after two weeks imprisoned in shoes. The sand gave softly under her weight and the shallow water, warmer than the air, licked around her toes and instep. The smell – of foam and seaweed and the dark odour of tar – was familiar, but always exotic and strange, always with a hint of otherness, a memory of far away.

A hundred yards ahead, a flock of gulls stood motionless at the tide's edge, each with its own reflection in the wet sand. They rose noisily into the air as she approached and she paused to watch them land again, further along the beach. Apart from the gulls, there was no living thing in sight. She was alone. On her left, the sea curled and foamed beneath the perfect sky and there was only blue. The colour of heaven, she thought, the colour of gentleness and sleep. On her right, the cliff rose, steep and black, the sand at its base littered with fallen rocks and flotsam and pitted with crevices and caves. Sometimes she entered and explored the caves, but not today. Today the sea was all-enticing. Today the feel of the sand under her feet and the touch of warm salt water was all she wanted.

'Eve!'

She spun around and he was running along the line of the tide to catch up with her. His hair flopped in rhythm with his running feet. She waited, watching his easy, pleasant grace. When he was within fifty feet of her, he slowed down to a walk. She could see his face, flushed from running. She could hear his panting breaths and her own breathing quickened to match his. It was Jake.

'What are you up to?'

'Nothing. Just messing around.'

'Me too,' he said, as he drew level with her. 'I might as well come with you.'

'Okay,' she said. 'Might as well … if you like.'

For a while they walked in silence, while he caught his breath. She waited for him to speak first. He never talked much. He was a quiet boy. He wasn't comfortable with words. She could tell. He lived his life without needing words. His thoughts were structured differently. She didn't want to frighten him away.

'Where are you heading to?' he said, at last.

She shrugged her shoulders.

'Nowhere. Just walking. Where do you want to go?'

He didn't answer. Instead, he picked a piece of driftwood off the sand and flung it out into the sea. She watched it spinning, white against the egg-blue sky.

'Did you see the seal?' he asked after a moment. He pointed back towards the cliffs.

'No.' She was curious. She hadn't seen a seal on this beach before. 'Where is it?'

He turned towards the cliff and she followed behind him. The sand below the cliff was littered with giant rocks – huge, hostile fragments, split from the crumbling face by tide and time, a chaotic echo of ancient storms. Jake clambered over the rocks and she followed close behind him … tense, silent, privileged because he was showing something only to her. They were sharing something secret on the empty beach.

He paused and pointed to a rounded shape wedged between two rocks. At first, it seemed to her like a large, grey rubber ball, squeezed out of shape and flattened by the rocks but, as she drew nearer, she could see the spreading tail and one limp flipper trailing on the sand. It didn't move. She crept closer, feeling a whisper of excitement. This was the first time she had been this close to a seal. She leaned forward and reached out her hand to touch it, then drew back, suddenly afraid. Tentatively, she stretched out one leg and pressed her foot against its side. She expected a reaction, movement, the warm resistance of skin and flesh. Instead, the shape yielded unpleasantly under her foot, a rubbery grey membrane … a slimy, water-filled balloon. She jumped back.

'It's dead,' she said, but Jake was already making his way back over the rocks. Of course it was dead. She should have known it was dead. Why else would it be here on the beach among the rocks at low tide? The sensation of the yielding, waterlogged flesh against her bare foot revolted her. The nauseating smell of dead flesh hung in the air and she was suddenly aware of the buzzing of flies. She turned away and followed Jake towards the sea.

'You didn't think it was alive, did you?' he asked.

She shook her head.

'Of course not. It couldn't be alive.'

'Once there was a whale,' he said. 'It wedged up here above the high tide. It lay here for weeks before it was washed away. It stank like shit!'

The dead seal haunted her as they padded down the slope to the sea but, in spite of that, she was elated. He had shared his secret with her. It was a sad, sour secret but she had shared it with Jake. They had seen it together. She watched him as he paddled out into the sea, the gentle waves lapping his bare feet and soaking his jeans. He picked up a tangle of leathery weed and spun it, lasso-like, over his head, then tossed it far out into the water. She liked to watch him. He was brown and compact, his movements graceful and fluid. He belonged to the sea, as the seal and the whale had done. It didn't matter to her that he didn't talk much. It only added to his beautiful strangeness. He didn't need words. His body spoke for him.

He turned and caught her watching him. For a moment, she was shy and embarrassed but she didn't look away. He smiled. He didn't often smile. He was a serious boy – troubled, tense – not like anyone else that she knew. Everything about him was strange. His life was different from her life. She knew that.

He came from Polperro, but he lived now with a foster family in the village. His life had been extraordinary. She had heard things. His parents hadn't looked after him the way parents usually did. He hadn't been sent to school. He had roamed the beach from dawn till dusk, fishing for crabs and digging for lost change in the sand, while his father and mother worked on the boats and drank in the pubs. It didn't sound so bad to her, but it 'couldn't be allowed to continue' they said.

He went to school now, of course, now he had been saved. She saw him every day at school – but he was different there. He didn't belong there. It wasn't his element. At school he was sullen and brooding, dark with silent anger. Here on the beach he was filled with light. His eyes, his sun-bleached hair and tanned skin. He shone with the glistening drops that clung to his face and his arms and legs as he splashed through the shallow water and she loved him. Absolutely and without question. She knew that she loved him.

'Let's walk right to the end of the beach,' he said. 'There's a cave that goes on for miles.'

'Okay.' She knew the cave. She had been there before, many times … but not with Jake. With him it was an adventure, something dangerous and wild. With him, it was completely and terrifyingly new.

It was a half-hour walk to the end of the beach. They walked in silence along the edge of the sea, trailing their feet in the warm salt water. Ahead of them, the gulls rose noisily and moved another hundred yards along the beach. She could see his feet padding the soft sand beside her own. The gentle autumn sun warmed their backs. She could hear the quiet thud of her heartbeat, echoing the rhythm of their steps. They walked a meandering path, sometimes close together, sometimes further apart. Once his swinging arm brushed against hers and she felt him tense and pull away. Now and again they paused to pick up objects from the tideline: a mermaid's purse, a cuttlefish bone, a green glass float that they hid among rocks to collect on the way back. The small waves sucked the sand at their feet and the whole day pulsed in a slow pendulum of movement and sound. Feet … waves … heart. It was a dream day. It was the best day of her life. It was the right day for a kiss.

The beach was a long, curving ribbon of sand ending in sheer cliff where the promontory thrust out into the sea. For a long time, as they walked, the promontory remained distant and small but finally it rose up, steep and sudden, as they neared the end of the beach. The cave was out of sight, hidden by rocks, but she knew exactly where it was. They both knew. Their pace slowed, as if by some unspoken agreement. She could feel his closeness as they dawdled towards the rocks. She stopped to pick up shells and he stood beside her, silently waiting. Overhead the kittiwakes screeched and reeled. The waves broke softly against the cliff. Everything else was stillness. She sat down on the sand and let the sounds and the silence fill her thoughts. He didn't sit beside her as she hoped but remained standing, looking out at the sea and the sky beyond.

This was a special place. She felt it and she knew that he did too. A meeting place of sea and land, of rock and air and water. The smell of tar and salt, familiar and strange, and behind them the waiting cave, damp and dark and hidden … a doorway into somewhere else, a crossing place between one element and the next. It had to be relished. It had to be taken a breath at a time – enjoyed, experienced. They didn't need words. They only had to be there. Then … after all this … would be the kiss. She knew it now. She was sure it would happen. It was just as she wanted it to be. This was the day when everything would change, the day when she would have been kissed.

'Do you want to go and look at the cave then?' He was standing behind her, his gaze still fixed on the horizon.

'Okay.' Her voice was barely audible.

He put out his hand to help her up. She took it and, when she had risen, their hands remained together, palm against palm, fingers intertwined, as they walked towards the cliff. When they reached the rocks, they separated and he clambered ahead of her. She watched his movements, animal and fast, leading her forward.

The entrance to the cave was a narrow gash in the face of the rock. Its black walls bristled with mussels and jewel-red anemones. Inside, the sound of dripping water echoed. They entered slowly, peering into the dim tunnel that stretched ahead. For the first twenty feet there was light enough to see but after that a turning led them into darkness. They walked on, deeper into the dark. She couldn't see at all now but the air was full of sounds: hot, wet, trickling sounds. She spread her hands out at her sides to guide her and the rocks were damp and strange with slimy, unseen textures. She hesitated. It was too dark. She hadn't expected it to be this dark. Ahead of her she heard his feet splashing through water, and the sound of his breathing in the darkness, but she couldn't see him at all. She listened for her own breathing and realised she was holding her breath. After a few moments, he stopped and there was only the sound of dripping water.

'We should have brought a torch,' he said. His voice was strange and hollow in this new, blind element. She glanced back towards the reassuring sliver of light that clung to the turning behind them. His feet splashed again, this time towards her, and she remained still, waiting, not knowing what to do. He came to a halt as he reached her. She could just make out his shape in the darkness. She could feel the warmth of him in the air around her. She could smell the salt on his skin. He was very close. They had only to move their heads for their lips to touch. Her heartbeat pounded inside her head. The slimy, living, unseen walls pressed in around her and all she could think – all she was sure of – was that she didn't want him to kiss her. Not now. Not yet. She didn't want it to happen. She wasn't ready for it to happen. She needed it to remain the thing she wished for and imagined. She wasn't ready for it to be real.

For a few moments, neither of them moved. The thick water dripped from the walls of the cave onto their faces and the noise of the sea thundered and echoed in the solid rock around them.

'It's freezing in here,' he said, at last. 'Let's go back.'

'Okay.' She turned towards the light and they made their way back to the entrance of the cave and the sun-filled air beyond.

The beach stretched back around the curve of the bay towards the village, wider now that the tide was at its lowest. Above their heads, the kittiwakes reeled and cried. The tide was turning and the sly waves crept up the slope of the sand towards the cliffs again.

'We can try again another time,' Jake said. 'We could bring a torch next time.'

She nodded.

'Okay,' she said. 'Let's do that.'

For a moment there was awkwardness between them. Then he smiled and pointed back along the beach towards the dunes.

'Have you seen the plane?' he said.

'The plane?'

'In the sand dunes. There's a rusty old bit of a plane half-buried in the sand.'

Of course she had seen the plane a hundred times before, but she shook her head.

'No,' she said. 'Show me the plane.' And together they set off along the slowly narrowing ribbon of beach.

A BIRD SO RARE

EMMA TIMPANY

THE HOTEL'S interior decor – the wood panelling in the dining room, the columns in the atrium, the startlingly beautiful carved mantelpiece in the bar – seemed charming at first glance. But as they sat down to afternoon tea, they noticed holes in the panelling on either side of the door revealing not, as they would have expected, an authentic heart of old oak beneath a time-grimed surface, but hairy strands of yellow fibreglass.

'Seeing that yellow is a little death,' Frieda said. She was beginning to doubt if the two male angels guarding the fireplace, which despite their benign expressions had hands ready to draw swords from sheaths, were the real thing either. When she had first seen those angels, she had wanted to run her fingers over their dark bronze curls. Now she was glad that she hadn't, that the illusion of finding some rare treasure had lingered a little longer than it would otherwise have done, that she hadn't made a spectacle of herself and given an audience to her disappointment.

'Does it matter, though?' Michael said. 'What difference does it make whether they're real or not?'

'It makes all the difference in the world. Better if the walls were painted white. The rooms left empty. Look at them. They're beautiful rooms.'

'Yes. Yes, they are.'

The ceilings were at least twenty feet high. French doors set into bay windows opened onto a terrace that looked over the sea of trees to the coast. In the far corner of the sands, the chimneys of the china clay works gleamed silver. They were a couple of what the locals called blow-ins, people who'd drifted westwards from up-country and stayed put. They'd been married for longer than that though, almost twenty-five years. They had met when young and stayed together while all around them, one by one, their friends' marriages and partnerships broke down. What's your secret? people asked them, but in truth there was no secret. They simply abided. Recently they'd had a bad patch. No particular reason; many small grievances had accumulated, each one cobweb light, until they had found themselves either with nothing to say to each other or shouting and slamming doors. This holiday was their chosen salve, agreed upon because they both liked walking and swimming in the cold, green sea.

On the way back to their room, they stopped by a board in the foyer displaying captioned photographs of rare types of plants and animals found, over the years, in the hotel woods and gardens: strange moths, rare butterflies, enormous unidentified grubs. The grounds of the house had an oddness to them, a forgotten air, as though time itself had somehow stalled halfway down this valley. Through the open doors, the voices of families echoed as they moved to the lodges scattered throughout the trees, and somewhere a group of sea shanty singers bellowed, their voices rising to the top floor and drifting in the open window to where Frieda lay afloat, footsore after their long walk, in a tepid bath.

By the time they made their way back downstairs, the singers were gone, the early evening barbeque packed away. Dodman Point lay white in the evening light. The waters of the bay, violet with late sun, were empty of boats. Arm in arm they walked from the terrace down past an organic vegetable patch and a butterfly garden before stopping by an enclosure containing half a dozen giant rabbits, surrounded by a fence too low to be any serious attempt to contain them.

'Look at them.' Michael gestured to the huge bodies. 'Natural born killers, each and every one.'

She knew what he meant, but chose to pretend not to understand him. 'You fear for your safety? Aren't rabbits vegetarian? Anyway, they're all asleep. Do you think we're allowed to go in and pet them?'

'Do you want to go in and pet them?' Michael folded his arms.

'No, actually. No, I don't.'

'The size of them. They're bigger than your average cat. One bite could take your finger off.'

He was right in a way. There was something disturbing about them, apart from their size. Was their lethargy a result of overbreeding? In her mind rabbits were small, quick, darting little things, masters of camouflage, barely glimpsed before they'd disappeared.

'What's wrong with this place? Why can't they have normal rabbits?'

'I've no idea.'

Though Michael's eyes remained fixed on the enclosure and didn't roam to the trees, she became aware that his focus had moved on. About him was a certain intensity of concentration, a quality of stillness, his head tilted over to one side, his body poised on the edge of sudden action. He had tuned in to something calling, sweet and high, in the darkening leaves. If she spoke to him now he would not hear what she said, so she whispered, 'Perhaps it's time we gave this up.'

When a few moments later he said, 'What was that?' she thought that perhaps she had been wrong, that he had indeed heard her, before realising that it was not she who was present in his thoughts. He was speaking of the bird which, unseen among the leaves, its call too brief to allow identification, had eluded him.

How does it feel, she silently asked the rabbits, to live with someone whose mind is always partly elsewhere, on whatever winged thing is within sight or sound? This time, the familiar anger fixed itself into a resolution. If he does this to me one more time, I will leave him. She was tired of arguing about it. Her mind flashed back to the time when she had been relating a piece of particularly bad news and his first comment had been, Look, woodpecker. She had grown used to his exclaiming suddenly, breaking off in the middle of a conversation to run to the window, realising now that it was not a sign of danger or distress but that the alarm calls of the rooftop gulls had alerted him to the flight of some raptor over the back garden. She felt no more for birds than she did for any other living things she liked; otters, for example, or hedgehogs. If forced to choose a favourite bird, she would probably pick the owl, symbol of wisdom and death, the good it promised inseparable from the evil it bestowed, as double-edged as the old gods of Mexico.

During dinner, the woman sitting at the table opposite them kept her pink iPhone raised to her face; a black eye shape on its back surrounded the camera lens. Even while she was eating, she moved the lens around the room as if she were filming everything. At another table a man, loud-voiced as the drunk or partially deaf, complained bitterly that though he'd been the second person to book a table for dinner, he hadn't been given one of a pair of window seats, haranguing the couple seated there, telling them that they had taken his place. Outside it was dark, and the doors had been closed against the evening chill.

'Busy tonight,' Michael said, not seeming to notice that they had barely spoken to each other since they had left the rabbit enclosure.

'These must be all the people we could hear earlier: the people in the trees. The room is completely full.'

'Yes,' Michael said, 'they couldn't squeeze anyone else in if they tried.'

So it was strange, the next morning, when they came down for breakfast, to find the dining room, but for themselves, completely empty. Inside her was a kind of clarifying calmness, the sort that comes, for better or worse, after a decision, long postponed, has finally been made. Now, when the moment came, all that was left for her to do was to act.

They chose a table beside the window. Morning light brightened the tops of the trees though the valley still lay in shade. The doors were open again and in drifted the smell of cut grass, green and soothing, mingling with the earth smell of the cooked mushrooms on her plate. As she raised her cup to her lips and sipped, the coffee's bitter milkiness began to warm and wake her. The sea seemed closer than it had done last night, but the black shapes of birds visible on its surface were safely distant, rising and falling with the waves' breath.

Michael began to glance repeatedly out of the window and back again. He took his glasses off and cleaned them on the thick, white linen napkin. It had come sooner than she had expected. She eased her knife and fork together on her plate, her appetite lost.

'What is it that you see?'

'What does it look like to you?' He pointed to the sparse top of a conifer, a naked-looking branch almost devoid of needles. The apex. It was the exact place on their Christmas tree where she always balanced the angel.

Caught in a net of light, a bird.

'Whatever it is,' she said, 'it's big. And it looks … golden.'

'Hmmm.'

A name came into her mind along with the image of a bird so rare that she had never thought to see one in her lifetime. As big as a thrush, the bird in the tree was motionless; its yellow plumage was black-edged, as if it had been carved from some dark wood and then, held delicately by its wings and tail, dipped in gilt.

'An oriole?' she said.

'It looks like one, but they're incredibly elusive. They don't just sit in trees out in the open like that.'

'This one does.'

'I can't be sure unless I go outside. Take a closer look.' He pushed his chair back.

'Michael?'

'What?'

'Michael, there's something we should …'

'What's the matter? You don't mind, do you?'

'Before you go, I think that we need to …' Across the path of her words, a shadow fell and what she had meant to say was lost in darkness. Long ago, she had read something about that ancient world of incessant substitutions, of weird metamorphoses. She had read that after his longest pursuit, in the sea off Rhamnus in Attica, Zeus had finally caught up with Nemesis: in the form of a swan, he had settled on her wild duck.

'What is it, Frieda?'

Greek mythology had once been a passion of hers, but it was a love that, with the passing of time, she had lost. The older she grew the stranger the world seemed, increasingly hard to comprehend as it actually was, let alone when it was covered in layers of leaky, elaborate myth. 'It's nothing,' she said. 'Nothing's the matter. I don't mind. Go on. Off you go.'

He walked out of the doors and along the grey slabs of the terrace.

When she felt ready, pushing back her chair, she went outside and stood beside him. In flagrant defiance of the men who wrote bird-watching manuals, the bird still sat at the top of the tree, exactly where they had first seen it.

'Well?' she said.

'I can't be sure without looking at it through binoculars.'

'You go and get them. I'll keep an eye on her for you.'

'If it is an oriole, it's probably a female. The males are more intensely golden.'

'Is that so.'

The moment after he stepped off the terrace, the bird took flight. Down she swooped, back into the cover of the top canopy, the place where she and her kind were known to cower; the place where, despite their extravagant colouring, they habitually eluded detection by even the sharpest-eyed of observers.

It took her a moment to register the change, her speed and grace as she skimmed through dappled forest light then up and out into the vast, unbroken blue. The next time she looked down, he was already far below her.

TOO HOT,
TOO BRIGHT

S. REID

A COVE

I WAIT for you as I have done these thirty years and more, listen for the brush of bracken along the path up on the cliff top. You are light-footed for a heavyset man. I catch the ghost of a fox cutting over the bank into the field. There have been foxes here all along, cubs in springtime. We are night creatures too, hiding from the light, not wanting to be caught.

You are late tonight and the cold starts eating into me even though it's June turning to July. Rooks gather in the dusk to drink at the meeting of the stream and the sea before flying up to roost. I wedge myself into a curve in a rock, turn up the collar of my jacket, listen to the pull of the waves.

We have mapped this cove, know where to find a flat edge seat, shelter from a sou'westerly, the upper reach of a spring tide. Not much of a moon tonight, just a crescent dipping out of the heavy darkness. We've always been careful, left no trace. No letters, no lantern, no torch. I've always kept myself to myself in that way.

It was difficult in those days. I used to go to chapel back then. Didn't think too deeply about it, not a great believer, but when I was in that musty granite hall, hymns filling every corner, I felt I'd got my feet on the ground, roots stretching down into the salty earth. It was your voice that caught hold of me. A fine baritone that growled into bass. Barrel-chested. I closed my eyes and let the sound wash through me.

We found this place by chance. A summer hike along the southern stretch, out past Penzer, Kemyel, Half Tide Rock. The stream crossed our path, falling from a spongy corner of a field down to the sea. We dipped our feet in the peaty water and followed its descent, catching hold of willow branches, our feet sliding on the rocks, down to a cove. A slither of shell sand cut through with bands of rock. Hidden. Safe.

I close my eyes and I can still catch the warmth of you, that first time.

I taught you how to fish in the early days. Agile then. Free as birds. We scrambled along the rocky arm, our feet catching on limpets and dog whelks, crabs and blennies hidden in the nooks. Out to deeper water on the point, out to cast a line from the jutting edge.

Our canvas shelter, on a ledge above the tide, tightly knit into the blackthorn, is more comfortable these days. Velvet cushions and a Turkish rug. Still I wait for you. Wrap myself in a woollen blanket. The waves are louder at night, knocking at the door when they are halfway down the beach. The lost chime of the Runnel Stone bell caught in the swell. Cold as winter, jack snipe feathery in the marsh.

*

Two weeks come and go, with no sign of you. Our time has a pattern – Wednesday night, if not this one then the next. This summer damp gets under my skin and aches creep through the joints of my wrists and fingers. I cannot settle even in my studio, perched at the top of my house, looking out across the mossy roofs and grassy chimney pots, across the reach from Lizard to Newlyn. The open window catches the calls of swallows flitting in Morrab Gardens below. I cannot paint and put the brush aside, the canvas all shapes and lines but no colour.

I have lived here for twenty years or so, loved this place from the moment I saw it. A tall, elegant, airy house, a window at each landing catching morning and evening light by turns.

In the kitchen, I switch on the radio and the jaunty songs of the local station jar the still rooms as I check again for any news of you – an accident perhaps. I phone the hospital but cut the call when a voice asks me for my name. Too risky. Even Martha, my long-legged black and white cat, is restless today, stalking from one room to the next. I need some air and walk through the gardens to the library.

The reading room is quiet, at rest, the hands of the clock on the mantelpiece held fast at ten to five. I pick up The Cornishman from the fan of periodicals on the table and scan the pages. Palms and ferns dapple light through the window across the carpet. And then, finally, in small neat type, I find it. Robert, beloved husband of Ros, devoted father to Rachel and Hannah. Funeral service to be held at St Mary's Church.

A CHURCH

THE NIGHT ticks by. Brittle sleep. I wake, fear racing, my body breaking into fragments. I tell myself I must attend the service or I will always be waiting for you at the shore. And yet I cannot face your wife, your girls.

I pick strands of rosemary, geranium, dew-wet, bind them with a string. I iron a shirt, polish shoes, sip coffee at the breakfast table.

Even now I step aside, put back the hour, avoid the time to come. It's early yet. I walk down Chapel Street, head out along the promenade, and breathe the seaweed air. High above herring gulls, lifted, rising, forty, fifty, maybe more, glinting morning stars.

Already early swimmers are queuing at the entrance to Jubilee Pool, open to the elements, cut into the rocks, and I join the line as the attendant draws open the iron gate.

Robert. This gentle pool, poster blue, cut through with a herringbone breeze, I run my fingers through your hair. These elegant curves, these steadfast rails, this ship of idling limbs and breaths.

A chilly slab to lay my clothes. The clip of water on the sides. I dive through the line from day to dusk, reach out and touch your skin. Silken salt in this drop of ocean. I no longer hear the herring gulls.

The orange buoy, the safety rope, the tolling of a bell.

I take a seat near the back of the church. The flowers lie limply at my feet. The pews set close upon each other. Water from the pool trickles down my hair, down my neck, dampens my shirt.

I hear the clip of shoes on stone, catch whispers.

Not at the chapel in Newlyn then?

His mother wasn't having that. High church. She had her way, of course.

And Ros?

Not happy. But not a lot she could do about it.

The service starts, and I grasp phrases here and there – beloved son, loving husband, devoted father – falling leaves.

My Robert. A slither of candlelight catches the copper band around my wrist. I touch the cool metal.

There was a lazy slack tide that night. I remember how you held me close. The warm smell of wood, sawdust in the pores of your skin, touched dusking raven hair speckled with grey.

You placed a small band of gold in my palm and closed my fingers around it. We're getting on a bit now, you said, Rachel and Hannah grown up and away. We could take our chance. And as we lay there, still as the night, my mind swithered this way and that. Finally, a life together, something I had not allowed myself to even hope for. But at what price? Ros and the girls, your family torn apart.

When you had told me, twenty years back it must be now, how you wanted more than us, a settled family life and children – Ros – I accepted that. Loved you still. To be honest, I'd never given them much thought, bracketed them away. I steered clear of the village, never asked you about them. Just a way of coping.

What about Brighton? You squeezed my hand. A flint house by the sea in Norfolk? Things are different now. People more accepting.

I pictured our domesticity – log fire in the winter evenings, deckchairs in the garden, a marriage bed.

You held me. Anywhere, Geoff.

A HOUSE

I SLIP out of the church, sit down on a bench. Dusty paths, a granite wall overgrown with valerian, ivy and bramble.

The mourners brace themselves in the sunlight as your coffin is lowered into the ground. I hold myself steady, cast the flowers into the grave. The girls lean into their mother, slender grasses blown in the wind.

I follow them, a stranger behind a crowd, walk these windings to

Newlyn. I cannot be alone right now, I cannot say goodbye just yet, and part of me just wants to see and know this other part of you.

The house barely holds us all. A press of bodies in a low-ceilinged room. I lean on the cool damp wall, adjust my eyes to the dim light.

A glass of brandy is pressed into my hand. A kindly, weathered face. Out of the blue, isn't it? Fit as a fiddle, he was, what with his work and all. Still can't take it in.

He searches my face, can't place me.

Ah well, he says and shoulders through the crowd.

Sweat prickles my back. I down the brandy, loosen my top button. I run my fingers across the dining table, the fine grain of the oak. We share a love for shapes and things – your wood and chisel, my paint and canvas.

A photo frame. Robert balancing the girls, one on each knee – they must have been around three and five years old when the picture was taken. I look for them across the room, look for Ros.

Spirits, wine, beer flow like water. I am knocking back brandy. Voices grow louder. The men sing the old songs, arms slung around each other's shoulders. The sound fills the room and presses against the walls. I close my eyes and hear your voice.

I gave that ring back to you, placed it in your hand. Too hot, too bright for me. We never spoke of it more, but it lay waiting, a life unlived. Perhaps it was her anger I feared most. Perhaps it was our secret splayed open in the light.

Ros sits on the window seat, on her own now, just an arm's length away. Frayed, all washed out. Strands of brown hair have come loose from the neat bun and curl limply onto her black velvet dress. Her gaze passes across me, unseeing, and shifts from one woman to the next, cousins, friends, neighbours. The room feels tight. My head swims. I have no place here.

I work my way through the rough tide, rolled this way and that. A whisky bottle scrapes hard along the bressummer beam and jags across the faint lines of the coffin drop. The hatch corners out of place and angles from the ceiling, heavy, falling. I am held fast in the swell and can only watch as it slides down towards me.

Voices, muffled, far away. Jesus Christ. Knocked out cold. Never seen him before. Give him some air. Get him upstairs so he can lie down. He'll be all right in a bit. I'm lifted. Floating. Nowhere.

There are twelve squares of glass in the window, twelve squares of grey light. The room spins.

Are you okay? A soft voice. Brown eyes looking into mine. I feel the weight of a hand on my shoulder. Ros. I close my eyes, shooting pain in my forehead.

Are you okay, love?

I force my eyes open. I'm all right.

She hands me a glass of water. Holds it as I sip. Her hands are cool. Mine slippery, clammy.

There now.

She leaves me, pulls the door to.

The bedspread is soft against my face. The pillow smells of you, of wood. I drift off, sense her presence in the room now and then, turn in my sleep.

It's quiet now downstairs. I sit up and steady myself. The room is darker now, dense with evening light. A dressing table, brush and comb neatly placed. A cotton scarf thrown across a chair. My jacket hangs on a hook on the bedroom door. I find my shoes under the bed and, as I bend forward to tie the laces, my hand catches on a crumpled shirt. I lift it to my face, and the thing is, it smells of me as well as you, of us. I hold it close, pressed tight into my eyes. Just breathing, in and out, and it feels like the first time I've been able to breathe all day. And then I hear the gentle click of the bedroom door.

THE WILD

I HAVE not gone back to the cove since you passed away. No doubt the foxes are still there, our shelter tatters in the blackthorn. Force myself to paint these days, try to keep a structure and routine, but find myself more often gazing out of the window, across the roof-tops to the bay. My palette is more muted, picking out softer tones. I tell you things I left unsaid, wish you back among the living.

Autumn now. Every day I head out and walk. The woods shelter me, wrap me round with a cloak of beech and oak and moss. Here I am nothing, invisible, safe. I walk between a broken wall of ancient granite stones and a stream that gathers pace as it falls through the valley. Black stalks of fungi snake up from softening wood.

I lie down in a shallow dip and look up through the branches to the milky sky. A blackbird rifles through the leaves searching for insects, a wren hops through the ivy. The stream falls into a beach of rounded boulders.

Ros stands at my door, cotton scarf, red rose pattern, wrapped around her neck and shoulders. She looks different, resolute, lost some of the weariness of that day. I had wondered if she would seek me out.

I offer coffee, biscuits. I'm all fingers and thumbs.

I kept looking till I found you, she says. I always knew there was someone.

I don't know what to say. I sit opposite her, awkward, feel I am a stranger in my own house.

Her gaze travels around the room, taking in the paintings on the wall, out through the glass doors to the garden.

We had a good marriage. Our children. Rob and I were happy.

She looks back to me. And so I tell her, how we met when we were barely twenty, how I loved you for more than thirty years, and how I miss you now.

And I hold back from her our beloved cove, the golden ring.

The early hours are the most difficult for me. They hold an ashen quality, before the waking day. I go upstairs to my studio and focus on my work. The ancient patterns of the woods, the subtle hues of bark and ferns, abstracted into lines and curves. They will ship to London, Berlin and New York early in the year.

I did not think I would see her again, and yet she returns in January, blown in with the gale.

I'm going out to Bosullow. Come with me, she says.

I glance at her in the car. Her hands are small, pale on the wheel. The car is old, the radio tinny. She has cut her hair. It's short now, stylish, curls around her ear.

We wind through Madron, past the poorhouse lane, park up on the moors. Love, duplicity, our quiet companions as we walk the high-hedged track. We cross the stream to Men an Tol, then up to Ding Dong mine. I follow her along the narrow path across the hollow earth. You wrap your arm around her shoulders, match her stride up the hill. Protective ghost.

We shelter by the crumbling wall and neither knows where to begin. The secrets, lies, the other life. Another body, another skin, resting here between us, lying still. A delicate thing, too raw to be picked over by small birds. Her eyes are darker than yours, a deeper chocolate brown. The wind is biting cold. My lips are numb. Our words are whipped away unspoken across the tops.

We walk along the ling-lined track to Nine Maidens and turn to lighter things. My exhibition in New York, Rachel at uni in Bath, Hannah working at the hospital. Sheltered Mount's Bay to the south. White caps and a boiling sea out past Long Ships to Wolf Rock.

Through that winter we walk. Mulfra, Grumbla, Pendeen Watch. When the wind is battering at the windows, the clouds hurled across the bay, I have a feeling she will come. And I wait for her, the ship's bell ringing out at my door. We become companionable in our quietness. We share a love of natural things, a badger track amongst the bracken, a kestrel stalking the cliff top edge.

I lean against a granite slab. Close my eyes and breathe the warm coconut of winter gorse. I feel her eyes upon me, mapping the details. My freckled skin, red hair, greying now, flecks of paint worn into the creases of my hands.

A BOOK UNREAD

THE RAIN. A walk along the promenade. Hand in hand. New lovers old as time. A dog skitters through the glassy puddles. Breakers belly over Battery Rocks, leap the railings and spray collapses on the low terraced houses.

At my back, the tower of St Mary's Church, staunch upon the hill. It's a year now since you passed away. Back in winter I dreamt you stood there, lost, waiting. Cold earth. Sometimes I allow myself to imagine us together. If I had been braver, stronger. Twist and turn the past this way and that.

Things are different now.

May had brought a heatwave, drawing hot dust from Algiers, Granada, Cadiz, tracing ancient trading routes. That day, a turning point. Too bright to stay inside and work.

I climbed down to Pedn Vounder, the beach curling into the cliff. The morning tide tight upon the sand, a line of mist riding low upon the water, an offshore current sweeping invisible across the bay. I swam out fast until the blood left the surface of my skin. Lines of sunlight piercing the haze to open up small glinting pools, and I drifted between them, closed my eyes, trusting, buoyant. Water soft as velvet.

I stumbled shivering back across the beach. Sunbathers dotted across the sand, angled towards the sun. A figure lounging on a beach towel near to mine. My hands and feet numb. An offered flask of tea. We talked of books and films and art.

Morning turned to afternoon. The outgoing tide opened up shallow lagoons and we waded and swam out to the sand bar late in the day. So shall we see each other again? Bold, direct, cards placed upon the table. I traced my fingers along the line of his collarbone and rested them there. His sun-warmed skin. Eyes iris blue.

David. I waited for him to finish work for the day at the library in town. A book picked at random from a shelf lay open on my lap, unread, and I watched him walk across to me, tall and lean, angular, shirt and tie, goatee beard.

It's easier now, three months in. We walk to Newlyn and beyond. Passing glances, curious eyes. His fingers thread into mine, still holding the nakedness of a lazy Sunday afternoon. His jacket pegged up in the porch, dishevelled pillows on the bed. More comfortable in my skin.

And we walk home, along the strand. The sea, the town, the church, the pool. My love, the light of day.

ON THE BORDER

TIM HANNIGAN

THE VALLEY was rapidly losing the light. Somewhere beyond the little church town of Luffincott, where a no man's land of soggy fields lay between twin banks of woodland, I laid out my bivvy bag at a bend in the Tamar. A pair of herons lifted lazily out of the fields and flew away to the north in the twilight, dropping a cushioned yard between each slow beat of their broad blue wings.

The mud at the water's edge was a Rosetta Stone of animal prints: the spiny Cyrillic of small wading birds, the rosebud pictograms of a fox, the sharp cuneiform slots of a deer and the spidery hieroglyphs of a mink.

I fell asleep to the uneasy rhythm of the river, right on the border.

The first people to cross the Tamar – when it was nothing but a river running between two granite moors, and when maps were held only in minds – came somewhere far back, beyond even the first wisps of myth-smoke. They had walked overland from Europe when there was no water in the way, and they passed me in the damp darkness as I slept: small, fur-clad groups of light-limbed Palaeolithic travellers, coming down out of the eastern woods with chipped chert hand-axes and withy staves, seeking the shallowest bend of the river and wading across, bare feet feeling for the stones in the murky shallows, clambering up the western bank with muddy legs and then fading like deer into the forest. They moved lightly, some ten thousand years ago, glimpsed in the uncut wildwood. They built nothing that would last longer than it takes wood and hide to rot, and left no tally of their numbers. They came meandering along streams and skirting the deeper woods, picking along seaweed shorelines, and overturning slabs of slippery black stone in search of shellfish. They edged back and forth with the shifting seasons, and at least one small group made it to the very end of the peninsula.

One day, on the final slab of level ground between Land's End and the western moors, one of their number mislaid a hand-axe: a cream-coloured hunk of stone, tapered to a crude point. Maybe it was left behind by mistake when they broke camp and moved back east. Maybe a rawhide binding snapped as they loped in file through the willow thickets and the loss was only spotted an hour later, as they began to drop down the southern slopes towards Mount's Bay – with bitter recrimination and a frantic retracing of steps, for there was no stone that they could chip to a cutting edge in this country, and they would have to do without for the rest of the season. Or maybe the owner went out alone to gather firewood and met the Beast.

Either way, the axe-head was lost for ten millennia before it came up with the old season's potatoes behind the plough in a field just off the Land's End road in 1959.

I slept on undisturbed as more moving bands waded across the shallow stretches of the Tamar. These Mesolithic groups were bigger and better clad, and they carried bundled babies and baskets of the black flint they had gathered on the south coast of Devon to cut into new tools as they travelled. Some of them camped out on the high ground in the summer months alongside Dozmary Pool and, sitting cross-legged on the shore outside hide shelters, they chipped arrowheads and knives. One or two of the broken blades fell into the pool and were lost in the cold, peaty waters.

The night rolled over me and the sheep settled on the far bank and the river slithered on to the south, and more and more figures were moving westwards out of the trees as the fifth millennium BC gave way to the fourth. They stepped lightly over my sleeping form and splashed down into the river with wolfish dogs loping at their heels and spears over their shoulders. A little way upstream a family group drove a trio of bellowing, coarse-coated cattle through the shallows. They were small, slight men and women, these Neolithic travellers, with artists' fingers and thin faces. But once they had climbed the far side of the Tamar Valley and fanned out in groups along the length of the peninsula – searching now not for a one-night campsite, but for some high defensive hill or a patch of level land with good grazing – they began to do something entirely new, something that bound them in a wordless bond to every stonemason who followed, and that fixed their culture in the landscape forever: they began to move the granite around.

On the hills – never at the highest point, always a little way off to the side – they raised monstrous megaliths that none of their successors would ever see fit to challenge. And then, when these cromlechs were ready, they filled them with burnt bones.

I woke once in the deepest part of the night. The sheep were silent, and something – the mink which had visited this spot before I arrived perhaps – went into the river with a plop. I opened my eyes and saw the Plough, hanging Damoclean in a squid-ink sky, just above my head. As I turned on my side, hitched the hem of the bivvy bag up over my shoulder and went back to sleep, the clock was creeping towards 2,000 BC and an ever-thicker progression of figures was flowing to the crossing point.

These were thickset, ugly men with blunt noses, heavy brows and short-barrelled forearms. They went thundering across the river dressed in coarse cloth, and pressed on through the trees along what was now a well-trodden trail. Most of them still carried the stone axes and flint arrowheads of the earlier centuries – better worked, perhaps, but little different in form. But, where a larger group came through, the leader might carry somewhere on his person a blade or a brooch or a bangle made of a new material, the colour of a ballan wrasse's scales, worked with chiselled lines and stained a little with verdigris at the edges.

They pressed west, up onto the high sweep of Bodmin Moor and out into the land beyond, and they went wild with the granite. They upended menhirs in broad circles and laid the first net of fields over the land in patterns that would last forever. And if the Dartmoor–Tamar–Bodmin ramparts were not yet a kind of border, then they must at least have begun to take some shady shape in their mind-map, for by now there were people heading back out of Cornwall, a two-way traffic churning the river and treading the banks around me to a slippery mush. Those heading eastwards were carrying tin, raised as black cassiterite fragments from the granite gravel of the moorland streams, and others were bringing it back westwards, smelted with lead and copper and beaten into leaf-thin moons of bronze for the necks of high-born ladies.

The night was moving into its final hours now. The sheep were starting to shift again, and there were yet more people coming down out of Devon along what could almost be called a road. They had finer cloth and harder swords. Their ilk had filled much of Britain and they belonged to the edgelands of a wider tribal culture that stretched across the great levels of old Europe, a loosely linked mass of peoples whom the reporters of Ancient Athens, far to the south-east and hunched over their writing desks between Doric columns, called the Keltoi.

They went past me in deep conversation, driving herds of oxen and pigs, and once they were over the moors they went away left and right, south-west and north-west, shouting out new names for headlands and hilltops in their own language – names which, with a little luck, a twisted vowel here and a crushed consonant there, might just make sense to those with a few words of Cornish two and a half millennia later.

It was almost dawn.

I woke in a rainstorm after a sleep of centuries. The raindrops were popping like gunfire against my bivvy bag, and I hitched the hood over my head and lay there, shivering. Eventually the pace of battle eased, and I wriggled out into a morning of funereal darkness. There was no wind, and the banks of conifers on either side were black. The immobile sky was the colour of an old mop, and the hedgerows were waterlogged rucks. Everything was utterly sodden, and the river was running with quiet fury.

I shook the water from the bivvy bag, ate a few slices of cheese and stale bread, tugged on damp boots, and walked away to the north, into the eastern strip of woodland.

I had not been walking for more than a couple of minutes when I came upon the house. It was a sturdy, two-storey cottage with a couple of outbuildings, deep in the wood. It was abandoned. Brambles had welled up out of the garden, blocking the way to the door in wiry rolls, and ivy was beginning to take the mortar to task. The trees seemed to be closing in on it, shuffling an inch or two closer on bound footings each night, readying for a final, crushing rush. The house had not been empty for long, for I could still see the odds and ends of domestic life amongst the long grass: a spare tyre, a wheelbarrow and a pair of red gas canisters, leaning against one another for support beside the kitchen door. But the woodland was urging it all swiftly to dereliction. The thought that I had slept little more than a field away made my scalp prickle. There were no curtains in the upper windows and I tried not to look at them too closely. I hurried on at the panicky top gear of walking pace.

In the grim witch-light, this stretch of country felt like it had been abandoned in the wake of some medieval ill-fortune. The wet fields were uncut, the paths untrodden and the flocks ungathered.

I came out of the wood onto a rain-scored yellow track between high hedges. Gust after gust of crows came winging over the hawthorns in an irate cacophony. There were dozens of them, turning, sweeping back on themselves: a portentous infestation of tar-black feathers in a seal-grey sky.

At the top of the rise the hedge gave way to a dew-beaded fence and I saw what had brought the birds here. A flock of water-logged sheep were shivering miserably in a long field, nervous black heads turned towards me. In the middle of the field, away from the huddling herd, was the carcass of one of their number. I could see a red ribcage rearing from a mush of wool and blood. The crows – there must have been a hundred of them at least – were turning over the field in a murderous vortex. I wondered how the sheep had died and why no one from the farm had collected the carcass, and a brief vision of the worst-case scenario for the cause of a lost Palaeolithic hand-axe formed behind my eyes. Again, thinking of my nearby camping spot, a pulse of unpleasant electricity ran over my scalp and down my forearms.

I hurried on. When I had gone a hundred yards I glanced back without stopping. The crows were falling out of the sky like black snow.

NOTES

TALK OF HER

Dorothy Pentreath (Dolly), a Cornish fishwife who lived in Mousehole, gained the reputation of being the last native speaker of the Cornish language. Her portrait was painted by John Opie and can be seen at St Michael's Mount. Dolly died in 1777 and was buried in Paul Church, just outside Mousehole. A granite memorial stone was erected for her in 1860 by Prince Louis-Lucien Bonaparte, nephew to the French emperor and a keen linguist. This memorial was later thought to be in the wrong position and was subsequently moved.

THE SIREN OF TREEN

The epigraph is taken from Franz Kafka's short story 'Silence of the Sirens', 1917, published in The Great Wall of China: Stories and Reflections (Schocken Books: New York, 1946).

I TURN ON MY OWN AXIS

In June 2014, this story was recorded as part of Audiotor: Minions Lament, an immersive storytelling experience on Bodmin Moor.

A BIRD SO RARE

In April 2015, this story was published in Takahē 84 and Over the Dam (Red Squirrel Press: Morpeth, 2015).

TOO HOT, TOO BRIGHT

A coffin drop is a hatch in a ceiling through which a coffin can be passed in a house where the staircase is tightly angled.

ACKNOWLEDGEMENTS

We were very fortunate in being able to feature the work of two accomplished local artists in this book. The four exceptional woodcut illustrations were created by Angela Annesley to reflect the following themes: Cornishware, Enchantment, The Heart of the Storm, and Sailors' Knots. Vita Sleigh, a graduate of Falmouth University's celebrated BA Illustration course, designed the book cover with both sensitivity and bravura. Further details about both Angela and Vita can be found in the list of contributors. We could not be more proud of their work.

The editors would like to thank Faisel Baig; Adam, Iris and Lauren Drouet; Patrick Gale and the North Cornwall Book Festival; Nicola Guy, our Commissioning Editor at The History Press; Pete Hamilton at St Michael's Mount; Ron Johns at The Falmouth Bookseller; Nigel Owen, Head of Illustration at Falmouth University; The Society of Authors and everyone at Telltales for the help and encouragement they have given us.

THE CONTRIBUTORS

PHILIPA ALDOUS
Philipa has lived most of her life in Cornwall. Her childhood was spent roaming the dunes and windswept cliffs of the Atlantic north coast. She now lives near Falmouth.

ANGELA ANNESLEY
www.ravenstongue.co.uk
Angela is a printmaker based near Land's End. Her hand-printed woodcuts capture the elemental forces of the southwesterly winds that sculpt the land, sea and skies of Cornwall.

CATHY GALVIN
Cathy published her second collection of poems, Rough Translation, in 2016 and was shortlisted for the Listowel Poetry Collection Prize in 2017. She has been awarded a residency at the Heinrich Böll Cottage, Achill Island and a Hawthornden Fellowship.

ANASTASIA GAMMON
Anastasia lives close enough to Bodmin Jail to hear the ghosts. She has a degree in English and Creative Writing and promises she'll finish a novel one of these days.

TIM HANNIGAN

Tim was born in Penzance. He is the author of several narrative history books about Southeast Asia and is currently working on a PhD at the University of Leicester.

CLARE HOWDLE

Clare lives in Falmouth where she runs a copywriting business. Her short stories have been published in newspapers and international journals and she's currently working on her first novel, set in Cornwall and Rhodesia (now Zimbabwe).

ADRIAN MARKLE

Originally from Canada, Adrian is a writer, editor and tutor now based in Falmouth, where he is working on his Creative Writing PhD with the University of Exeter.

TIM MARTINDALE

www.timmartindalewriting.com

Tim is a writer, living and working in West Cornwall where he was born. He holds a PhD in Anthropology from Goldsmiths College and is a graduate of the Creative Writing Programme, Brighton. Currently he is working on a book about home, belonging and wayfinding.

CANDY NEUBERT

Candy's work has appeared in OUP and Virago anthologies, New Welsh Review and on Radio 4. She is the author of the novels Foreign Bodies and Big Low Tide (Seren) and a regular poetry contributor to The Spectator.

FELICITY NOTLEY

Felicity lives in Falmouth. She holds an MA in Creative Writing from UEA, where she was awarded the Seth Donaldson Memorial Trust Bursary. She was shortlisted for the Bridport Prize in 2015.

SARAH PERRY

Sarah grew up in Cornwall and is interested in personal stories of health and wellbeing. She has been experimenting with short story writing and enjoys reading at Telltales live literature events.

S. REID

S. Reid grew up in West Penwith, settled in Scotland and New Zealand, and currently lives in Falmouth.

ALAN ROBINSON

Alan is a writer and blues musician, festival performer, author of short fiction, short film, community theatre works, radio and stage drama. His novel, The Studio Couch and the Sand-Dancer Blues, is available online.

VITA SLEIGH

www.vitasleighillustration.com
Vita studied in Falmouth – the sea is a deep inspiration and recurring metaphor in her illustrations. Both Cornwall and creative writing are close to her heart.

ROB MAGNUSON SMITH

Rob is the author of The Gravedigger and Scorper. Recently his short fiction was selected for a compilation of audio recordings by Jeremy Irons. He lives in Falmouth.

KATHERINE STANSFIELD

Katherine grew up on Bodmin Moor and now lives in Cardiff. Her debut poetry collection Playing House is published by Seren. Her new novel The Magpie Tree is out with Allison & Busby.

EMMA STAUGHTON
Emma was shortlisted for the Bristol Short Story Prize 2015 and longlisted for the Bath Short Story Award 2016. She holds an MA in Creative Writing from Plymouth University and has just completed a collection of contemporary Cornish-based stories.

SARAH THOMAS
Sarah traces her ancestry to women who worked the farmland of Penwith and is interested in our relationships with place and landscape. She is currently working on a collection of poetry.

EMMA TIMPANY
Emma was born and grew up in southern New Zealand. Her previous publications are the short story collections Over the Dam and The Lost of Syros. She lives near Truro.

TOM VOWLER
www.tomvowler.co.uk
Tom's debut story collection, The Method, won the Scott Prize, and his novels include What Lies Within and That Dark Remembered Day. His latest book, Dazzling the Gods, is out now.

ELAINE RUTH WHITE
Elaine writes for page, stage and broadcast and has worked on projects for English Touring Opera, Bike Shed Theatre and the BBC. She also writes non-fiction as Elaine Farrell.

telltales

Telltales is a live literature event based in Falmouth, Cornwall and has been motivating, showcasing and inspiring writers in the South West since 2008.

www.telltales.org.uk